FIVE FORGOTTEN STORIES

In the winter of 1934–1935, according to H.P. Lovecraft's *The Haunter of the Dark*, Robert Blake had settled down alone, to work . . . He had painted 'nameless, unhuman monsters', and 'profoundly alien, non-terrestrial land-scapes' — and also, we are told, written five short stories, later believed lost. However, an exercise book, which belonged to a certain 'Robert Blake' of Providence, has been recently acquired — the contents, when deciphered, appear to be five weird tales . . .

JOHN HALL

FIVE FORGOTTEN STORIES

Complete and Unabridged

LINFORD
Leicester

First published in Great Britain

First Linford Edition
published 2009

British Library CIP Data

Hall, John, *1946 Apr. 24* –
Five forgotten stories- -
(Linford mystery library)
1. Horror tales, English.
2. Large type books.
I. Title II. Series
823.9'2–dc22

ISBN 978–1–84782–789–0

Published by
F. A. Thorpe (Publishing)
Anstey, Leicestershire

Set by Words & Graphics Ltd.
Anstey, Leicestershire
Printed and bound in Great Britain by
T. J. International Ltd., Padstow, Cornwall

This book is printed on acid-free paper

To:
Paul M. Chapman and
Colin P. Langeveld

Contents

Introduction

Having sent home for most of his books, Blake bought some antique furniture suitable for his quarters and settled down to write and paint — living alone, and attending to the simple housework himself. His studio was in a north attic room, where the panes of the monitor roof furnished admirable lighting. During that first winter he produced five of his best-known short stories — The Burrower Beneath, The Stairs in the Crypt, Shaggai, In the Vale of Pnath, *and* The Feaster from the Stars — *and painted seven canvases; studies of nameless, unhuman monsters, and profoundly alien, non-terrestrial landscapes.*

The Haunter of the Dark by H.P. Lovecraft; first published in *Weird Tales* in 1936.

Astute readers will recall that in the winter of 1934–1935, Robert Blake

1

— whose last days are recorded in H.P. Lovecraft's *The Haunter of the Dark* — wrote five weird tales (for the uninitiated, I have reproduced the relevant paragraph above). These were believed lost, but recently I acquired an old exercise book, which belonged to a certain 'Robert Blake' of Providence, has been reliably dated to the 1930s, and appears to have taken sixty-odd years to make the journey from his hands in Rhode Island, New England to mine in Yorkshire, old England. Although it is impossible to verify the identity of the author beyond a reasonable doubt, the book contains outlines for five tales with the titles mentioned by Lovecraft.

The content of the stories has been somewhat difficult to decipher. Not only are the notes written in a mixture of shorthand (evidently of Blake's own invention) and the ancient Akkadian script, but they are also liberally interspersed with alchemical and what I imagine could be called 'necronomical' symbols. The gist, however, seems clear enough, and these present tales are offered as my own attempts to reconstruct them.

John Hall
Leeds, 2008

The Stairs in the Crypt

In the spring of a year late in the 1920s, a young man named Howard Phillips took the lease of an empty house in a little old town in Arkham County. The Depression was not properly over, and the property was cheap; not that it mattered to Phillips, who was a rich man, despite his youth. The house appealed first to his sense of the curious, as being ancient and ramshackle, but it was large and comfortable as well.

Phillips did not mix much with his neighbours, but pursued his obscure academic interests amongst his own books or in the library of the university in the city twenty miles off. And indeed he had few neighbours, for many of the young folk had left the little town to seek their fortune elsewhere.

There was a small church at the end of the lane on which stood Phillips' house, and Phillips attended the morning service every Sunday, partly because this was the only time he saw his neighbours, and partly because of the love of the curious which marked his character. Certainly it was not from any strong religious conviction — which, truth to tell, would have sat ill with some of his researches. The church dated from the middle of the seventeenth century, and was dedicated to St Michael and All Angels, a circumstance which itself intrigued Phillips, quite apart from the quaint architecture and decoration. The only slight drawback was the pastor, an aged man much given to stern warnings about the fate in store for sinners. Then, too, there was a stout oak door which evidently led to a crypt; this door was closed with a chain and padlock, and old Pastor Hayes refused point-blank to let Phillips explore the crypt.

The sexton, a man named Oakmore, as old as the pastor and as fervent in his religion, stood nearby whilst Phillips sought, and the pastor refused, the necessary permission. Oakmore was a near neighbour of Phillips in the little lane, and he walked the few score of yards back home with him. 'Pastor's right,' observed Oakmore, as they walked. 'I know you young chaps won't have it, but us old 'uns know there's things that should be left undisturbed.'

Phillips very naturally asked, 'Why?' and 'What?' and so forth, but got no satisfactory reply.

So matters stood in the autumn of that year, when an outbreak of influenza swept the little town. Most recovered, but Pastor Hayes succumbed. Now, although Phillips was not what we might call religious, he knew two men who were. One, his uncle, lived in the city and was high in the general assembly of the congregation which the pastor had graced. The other, the Reverend Mr Green, was an old friend of Phillips' from his school days, and was currently helping to run a shelter for the less fortunate in another, larger, city in another state. It was an easy task, then, for Phillips in effect to arrange for Green to take over the custody of the parish.

'You'll find things different here, Tom,'

said Phillips, as they stood together outside the church.

'Indeed, it looks peaceful enough.' Green found as he lit his pipe. 'The dedication intrigues me; St Michael and All Angels is common enough in England, mainly on old pagan sites, but not that usual over here. I should not have thought the place was old enough to have a pagan site.'

'Witchcraft, perhaps, though I never heard of it here?' mused Phillips. 'Or an Indian sacred place, something of that sort? Intriguing. And, by the by, there is an old crypt in the church . . . '

A week or so after Green arrived, then, we see the two of them, with old Oakmore hovering in the background, making 'Tsk! Tsk!' noises, unlocking the rusty padlock, and taking off the heavy iron chain. With some trepidation, and the aid of flashlights, they went down the duty steps.

'There's a light switch,' said Green doubtfully. 'Must have had electricity laid on almost when it was invented!'

Needless to say, the light did not work.

But their flashlights showed a cardboard box with bulbs of an old-fashioned sort in one corner, and — with a chair and much mutual advice — they put in a 'new' bulb, and tried again. This time the light came on, and they took a look around.

I do not know just what they had expected; skeletons, coffins, instruments of torture from the days of the witch trials, perhaps. What they saw was this: the ceiling was painted a deep blue and marked all over with silver stars arranged into constellations — though none that either man had seen before. There seemed, indeed, to be zodiacal imagery, but there were thirteen — not twelve — divisions, and again these were not entirely familiar. Here was Cancer, to be sure, or something very crab-like; but next came a constellation shaped like the classical dragon; and next a panther, or perhaps jaguar. In the darkest corner, too, was a cluster of stars that formed a strange and pretty well obscene figure of an hermaphroditic human; and next to that, a curious thing that looked like an octopus or devil-fish.

The walls, every one, were painted, covered with great murals that had evidently been inspired by the church's dedication, and had equally evidently been painted in the last quarter of the previous century. Angels, their wings protruding from the Pre-Raphaelite notion of medieval armour, fought and vanquished devils, imps, and demons beneath scrolls and banners bearing suitable biblical texts in Gothic script. Some of these imps and demons, too, were passing strange. Some were conventional enough, but in dark corners — overshadowed by the angelic figures, and sketched so lightly as to be difficult of distinguishing accurately — lurked curious things that would puzzle any student of marine flora and fauna. And some that would bring a shudder of horror to the most prosaic.

The masterpiece was on the wall furthest from the steps by which they had entered the crypt. Here was St Michael himself, almost twice life size, clad *cap à pie* in silver armour and with gold sparks shining from the blade of his drawn sword, which was engraved all over with strange patterns. The saint stood before an archway, beyond which was a staircase. But the perspective was odd; the viewer seemed to be looking vertically down the stairwell, and the stairs seemed to twist and turn, and to go down to infinite depths. The staircase was not empty; in the turnings and corners, dimly sketched, were more of the strange unearthly figures that could be seen here and there on the walls.

'Guarding the gate of heaven, perchance?' hazarded Green. 'Letting the faithful in?'

Phillips muttered something like, 'Or that of hell, keeping — others — out?' He laughed shakily when his friend turned to look at him.

'Well, it's spectacular, all right,' said Green, 'although some of the folk I've met here might not approve. And, indeed, I'm half tempted to have some bits painted out — '

'Oh, no!' said Phillips, who had a hatred of vandalism. 'A false ceiling, if you must, or just keep it locked up.'

'Hmm. Later; for now, I'll have to see

about some screens, and arrange the lighting. Yes, and some bunting, that will do very well.'

'For what?' asked Phillips.

'Why, for my Nativity, of course. This is the very place, a little straw, a few 'flats' — painted scenery, you know — and this will be the very stable!'

'Begging your pardon, sir?' This was Oakmore, who had followed them down reluctantly, and who could contain himself no longer. 'It might not be my place, sir, but — well — I wouldn't bring no children down here.' When they asked why not he took refuge in, 'Damp, sir. Damp and airless. Especially after the 'flu,' he added persuasively.

Oddly, Phillips tended to agree with the sexton. 'It is a touch mephitic,' he argued. 'And the subject matter of the paintings, and all.'

But Green had his heart set on a Nativity. There were just enough children in the little town to do it properly, and he set to work. There was but one baby, that of Mrs Van Neumann, who refused outright to lend it; but Green made shift with a rag doll, owned by Sukie Walters, who refused to be parted from it. Sukie was thus made the Virgin Mary, whilst Patsy Norton, who had filled that role, became a wise man, a demotion which she accepted without demur on condition that she had a beard which would sweep the floor.

The first week of December was clear and bright, and one Saturday morning Phillips attended a rehearsal. The cast was depleted, for there was some junior sporting fixture at a school in the next parish; but Sukie was there, and Bobby Turner, in his wise man costume though he had been told it was not a dress rehearsal, and a couple of shepherds.

'Mostly to get the scenery right,' said Green, wielding a paint brush and moving certain painted boards here and there. He gestured with the brush. 'Oh, sorry! Turpentine will fix that. I've left St Michael, you see, I thought him quite appropriate. And safe,' he added, glancing at the four of five children nearby.

Phillips strolled over to the great mural, wanting another look, for he had not

— for some reason — been into the crypt since he and Green opened it up.

As he looked, it seemed to Phillips that the artist had been highly skilled, in a perverse sense. The perspective of the stairs was almost three-dimensional, so that Phillips felt a distinct uneasiness, a vertigo, as he gazed into those infinite depths. Indeed, the ground seemed to shift, making him stagger slightly. He put his hand on the wall to steady himself — only it seemed to him that there was no wall there. Phillips hastily stepped back, and turned away — with a struggle, for the effect was quite hypnotic.

'All right, old man?' Green asked him.

'Yes, just a bit faint, or something. A bit close in here. Tom, did you feel anything . . . odd . . . just now? A tremor, something of that kind?'

Green frowned, and shook his head. 'Most probably the pipes for the central heating,' he said, for the church was heated by a strange antique arrangement of stoves and pipes, which Green had already grown to hate. 'I've noticed it before.'

'Tom, I'll have to go outside and get some air. Look here,' Phillips added reluctantly, as he made for the stairs, 'I don't know that I'd want a child of mine down here for very long.'

Green looked at him, but said nothing. Phillips went up the stairs, and out into the churchyard. As he leaned on an ancient gravestone, trying to collect his wits, he felt a peculiar sensation. Almost he could have sworn he heard a low rumble; almost he could have sworn that the ground shifted once more beneath his feet.

Old Oakmore happened to be digging up weeds in a corner nearby, and he too looked towards the church, a curious look on his face.

'You felt it too?' It was said before Phillips could think about it.

Oakmore nodded, silently.

'We'd best take a look.'

And they did. First the two of them, then the sheriff, then the county police; then the strange, silent men from Washington, who hid their identity behind mysterious groups of initials. The crypt, of course, was empty; of Green, and the children, there was not the least trace.

When the official investigation was over, Phillips persuaded his uncle to let him take a look at the crypt. Assisted by Oakmore and a couple of sheriff's men, he broke down the wall on which St Michael and the staircase were painted.

Behind the bricks they found a stone arch of great antiquity; and beyond that, another flight of stairs — only seven of them — ending in a solid block of stone. Not 'stones' in the sense of a wall, with cement and what have you, but a single, huge block of some black stone. From a distance it looked like a close-grained granite, but up close had the appearance of obsidian; certainly their crowbars could not put a scratch in it. There they had to stop, and perhaps it is as well.

Oh, and on the bottom step they found a rag doll, which they recognised. They told one another that it must have been in the crypt, unnoticed, and that one of them had knocked it into the excavation; but they said this with lowered voices,

16

and no conviction, and they did not look at one another as they said it.

Phillips moved away soon after. And others, too, the parents of the missing children especially, thought it best to move to new surroundings. So the little town did not long survive after the strange incident. Old Oakmore was one of the last to go, headed for his nephew's place in Idaho. As he made to get into the truck that was taking his few sticks of furniture, he looked at the church — now pretty much derelict — and muttered that some things were better left alone. The driver, an uncultivated man, merely spat out his quid of tobacco and reflected that the old man was rambling.

Shaggai

Picture postcard (depicting Dunchester cathedral, postmarked Little Snelling) from the Rev. Mr Hamish McLean to Mr Edward Lawrence, of Boston, USA:

Docken Magna, 2 Aug 1907

Dear Teddy,
Arrived yesterday after <u>long</u> journey via Dunchester, etc. No picture postcards of this place, nor yet a post office, nor a Dr — no sort of society at all — though there is an inn (of sorts), which I don't think I'll be patronising. I'll post this in Snelling tomorrow, and write properly soon. Trust you and family all well.

Regards,
Hamish

*From Mr Edward Lawrence to the
Rev. Hamish McLean, The Vicarage,
Docken Magna:*

Boston, August 28, '07

Dear H,
Many thanks for the p/card. No inn, no medical man, no Post Office, no society? My dear old chap, you really seem to have found either a rural idyll dreamed of by many and attained by few; or, the very back of beyond! You must write and let me know which it is. What about tobacco? Shall I send a few pounds of bright Virginia? I was talking with Peter M yesterday — you recall him from Oxford? — and he sends you his best. I think he intends to write; I passed on your new address. Ran into P quite by chance at the club, he's over here attending some symposium or other, I gather, and also looking up American friends, etc. Seriously, no inn? Still, as a man of the cloth (I suppose I shall have to start calling you 'Reverend' as we do over here) you won't need that sort of thing: <u>O, tempora, o</u>

mores, as old Prof T used to moan! Do you see the old Oxford crowd at all, or is it too isolated? By the way, Mother sends her regards, as does the old man, etc., etc.

Teddy

From the Reverend Hamish McLean, currently at Docken Magna, to Mr Edward Lawrence at Boston:

The Vicarage, Docken Magna,
18 Sept, 1907

Dear Teddy
Thanks for yours received yesterday. Did it come by one of the new fast passenger liners? It seems to have arrived very quickly.

As to this place — well, frankly, I have to say it's more 'the very back of beyond' rather than your imagined idyll! The place in and of itself is all very well — trees, fields, etc., 'as advertised' — but nothing in the way of entertainment. And nothing much by way of congregation, I regret to say. A few rather nice refined old ladies, and one or two of the local farmers and their folk, etc., but the labouring classes seem reluctant to turn up. Although possibly it's just the new man in the vicarage they mistrust? We shall see!

The village itself is a tiny place, a hamlet, I suppose you'd call it? A score of houses at the outside, though half a dozen farms with cottages and such in the parish, which swells the numbers a bit. Still, I don't believe there are more than two or three hundred souls in my care, which makes me feel rather a fraud, by the way, or would if this place were not so [here a word begun and evidently hastily scratched out] desolate. That is, perhaps, unfair on the place. After all, a good many rural parishes are thin on the ground these days. As the people move to big cities, lured by the prospect of streets paved with gold, etc. (The usual thing!) With company, of course (and that of the right sort) one might feel more at home. There is — I must tell you this! I forgot to say the nearest village is Little Snelling, with a Post Office — just a little shop and

General Store all rolled into one, but sells stamps and takes parcels, etc. Little S (called 'Snelling' by us all here) is 5 miles off; then Great Snelling (called 'town', would you believe it, as in 'we're bound into town') is 12 miles off, with the Dr and the nearest Vicar. A long walk, I managed it in a couple of hours, but was sweating profusely at the end, it being a hottish day (I'll hire a pony and trap from the inn next time). Dunchester is 35m off, a real expedition, and an overnight stay if one goes there. I passed thro' on my way here, and found a rather nice 'calabash' pipe — a bit dusty, looked as if it had lurked in the tobacconist's window since the Boer War ended — but a good smoker. The inn here sells tobacco — of a kind! But the newspaper shop in Snelling has promised to order me supplies from London.

Anyway, I lost my thread rather — doesn't matter! The Rector of Great S, Dr Hastings (D.D., very grand, I thought it was only bishops that had D.D.s) has a daughter, <u>Marie</u>. A pleasant and lively young lass, with very fine eyes and a magnificent singing voice. I might as well tell you, Teddy, she has pretty much stolen my poor old heart! Once things settle down — you know I have no family, or any money to speak of — but once I have saved a little, I plan to ask Dr H if he is agreeable to the match. Will you be my best man? Serious work afoot, old chap! I mean to make a will, and to be very grown-up about things. One must, after all. I'm 27 next year, and it's time to think about settling down . . . etc., etc.

From Mr Edward Lawrence to the Rev. Mr Hamish McLean:

Boston, October 17, '07

Dear H
  Many thanks for your letter and <u>hearty congrats</u>!!! Though I suppose it's still pretty much a secret? I might as well say that I, too, have been thinking seriously of matrimony, and intend to ask a certain Miss Dorothy Lathom if she'll have me! That is, assuming things go well — we are

both asked to spend Christmas with the Rawlingses (Mr and Mrs Rawlings, of Washington. I think I mentioned their son — Charles — who is a friend of mine). If things go well — well! You did rather skate over your promise, expressed or implied, to describe your new abode. Do let me know what the place is like. Fishing, you say? Would I like it . . . etc., etc.

From the Rev. Mr Hamish Mclean to Mr Edward Lawrence:

The Vicarage, Docken, 2 Nov 1907

Dear Teddy

I trust all goes well with Miss DL at Christmas!

Yes, I meant to describe the village and etc., though the other news was, I thought, too good to keep to myself! Docken (Magna added on maps, but left out in ordinary speech <u>ut supra</u>) is as I've said: tiny. There is (or was) a Docken Parva, which must have been minute in the extreme. Nothing there now, just a few hummocks in a field belonging to one of the farmers. It might, perhaps, repay a little amateur archaeological work next summer. Can you get over and I'll lend you a shovel? The field, by the way, is very rough and weedy. I asked the farmer and he shied away; I more or less get the idea that the place is pretty much avoided because it's regarded as <u>haunted</u>, or used by witches, etc. This from one of the farmer's men, in exchange for 6d and a fill of my tobacco (at which he turned up his nose, it being a bit 'gentle' as he said). Very interesting! And, of course, it makes me all the more determined to investigate the place and its history.

I must add that it's all the more intriguing because this place — or the people, I should say — is a very hotbed of superstition. I mean, we all throw spilt salt over our shoulder, etc., but you would scarcely credit the diverse taboos you find here! Not cutting one's nails on a Friday, not having knives crossed on the table — all very ordinary, but they take them quite seriously and feel threatened if they miss anything out. Then there are also others, peculiar to the place, for eg. Certain trees are regarded as unlucky and there is the farmer I spoke of — though a ruined village might reasonably be expected to be regarded as haunted. I suspect this arises from the place having no Dr or other medical man. We have a midwife of sorts — a 'wise woman', I think the anthropologists would style her — and a sort of 'wise man', an old chap who doctors the sheep and cattle etc. with herbs and the like. And the humans, too, I shouldn't wonder! I've seen him come out of a few hovels, and the folk look guilty when you ask what's amiss. He — Mr Oldman (no joke) — actually cured a cold of mine which had been dragging on ever since I got here. Herbs — ugh — a foul-tasting brew, but strangely and wondrously effective! No wonder few folk bother with the Dr in 'town' (i.e. Gt Snelling).

Oddest of all, there is a curious old — 'statue' I suppose you'd call it — a stone figure, a 'graven image', almost, if I were superstitious myself. A strange thing, much weathered, so that it is difficult — downright impossible, to be plain — to see what it may originally have represented. Squat, with more arms or legs than seems called for. No features visible on the 'face', if that's what it is (or was). There did seem to me to be some sort of inscription on the base, though indistinguishable to a hasty glance. I tried the old brass-rubbing technique, which, as you know, can bring things up, and it reads: 'SHAGGAI'. What do you make of that? I can only think it must be 'S' for 'Saint', which the Roman church uses, but what of 'Haggai' — if I am reading it right — an OT prophet, one of the shorter fellows? Not, as far as I am aware, a saint though! I must find a RC priest and make further inquiry. I did take the trouble to ask Mr Oldman and one or two of the older (pun intended) parishioners about it, and — as so often here — they rather shied away! I forgot to say that the local 'squire' as I suppose he must be, is a Mr Partridge (again, I'm not making this up) — and he told me (very seriously) — that the statue was intended to 'keep the Evil One out of the church'. So, yet another local superstition!

As to the fishing . . . etc., etc.

From Mr Edward Lawrence to the Rev. Mr Hamish McLean:

Boston, December 1, '07

Dear H

Your new abode sounds like a veritable witches' coven (is that the right word)! Your 'statue' sounds <u>fascinating</u>. Yes, you must find a RC priest and ask him what it might be.

Christmas is fast approaching, have you any plans for the holidays . . . etc., etc.

Transatlantic telegram from Messrs Morton, Morton, and Balsam, solicitors, Great Snelling, to Mr Edward Lawrence (this having arrived with the above in the post):

Great Snelling GPO, 3:12 pm,
5 December, 1907
MR LAWRENCE DEEPLY REGRET
YOUR FRIEND OUR CLIENT THE REV
MR HAMISH MCLEAN DIED SUD-
DENLY YESTERDAY STOP LETTER
FOLLOWS STOP JAMES FRANCIS
MORTON MORTON AND BALSAM
STOP

'Mr Lawrence? Delighted, sir! Though, of
course, the circumstances are — ah
— considerably less pleasant than either
of us might wish. Sit down, sir. A cigar?'
Mr James Francis was not exactly Teddy
Lawrence's notion of an English country
solicitor, being only a year or two older
than Teddy himself. He smoked a pipe,
wore rather loud tweeds, and sported a
luxuriant moustache. Teddy, had he not
known otherwise, might have taken Mr
Francis for a turf accountant in a
flourishing way of business.

Teddy sat down in a slightly worn but
very comfortable chair. 'Thanks, I'll stick
to my pipe, if you don't mind?'

Francis raised his own old Peterson. 'A

pleasure to meet a fellow addict! I may say, some of my clients — well, I have to open the window before they condescend to open their hearts.' He looked down at his desk, and grew serious. 'I have not yet expressed my condolences, or not in person — '

Teddy waved this aside. 'That's understood, and anyway your letters were more than gracious.' There had been a busy time for the postal services with a minor flood of correspondence — though of a fairly impersonal nature — back and forth, before Teddy himself had arrived early in the new year at Great Snelling, and sought out Mr Francis. 'Your telegram naturally did not — could not — elaborate as to the manner of poor Hamish's death,' Teddy went on, 'and you have, to be blunt, rather evaded the questions I put to you on the subject in my various letters.'

Francis looked a little embarrassed at this, but said nothing.

Teddy continued, 'I appreciate that, inasmuch as we had never met, you knew nothing about me, and would perhaps not wish to say too much to a stranger. However, you will understand that, as Hamish's oldest friend, or one of them, and since he has no family of any kind . . . ' Teddy broke off, feeling he had lost his thread. 'Anyway, what I mean is, I'd very much like to know some of the details. Just for my own satisfaction, if that word is appropriate.' He hesitated once more. 'It just seems to — well, so very odd. Hamish had, as far as I'm aware, never suffered from a day's illness or anything or the like in his life. It was, I take it, a tragic accident? Unless it was some sudden seizure, but I cannot believe that.'

'Tragic? Yes, tragic.' And Francis made a great business of attending to his pipe, though it was burning perfectly well.

'Well, then?'

Francis blew a cloud of rank smoke at the ceiling. 'Mr Lawrence, I understand your concern, my dear sir. Indeed, I do. However — you will, I'm sure, excuse my being evasive again — but I should be grateful if you would not press the matter.'

'Oh?' This was, of course, guaranteed to make Teddy want to press the matter, and it showed in his face.

Francis sighed. 'As his solicitor — and since he had no family — there was an inquest . . . '

'Yes?'

'Well, I viewed the body.' Francis paused, as if reluctant to continue.

'Please be plain, Mr Francis,' said Teddy, a touch of impatience in his voice.

'Very good. The expression on poor Mr McLean's face — I mean, one hardly expects a man who has just died to look happy — but, well, I have never seen such a dreadful expression on any face, living or dead.'

Teddy frowned. 'Pain, you mean?'

Francis hesitated, apparently seeking the right words. 'That, yes. Not pain alone, though, but the sheerest mortal agony. And there was more even than that. There was surprise, but also something else.'

Teddy shook his head. 'I don't follow you, sir.'

'Horror,' said Francis shortly. 'It sounds strange, I know, but that's the only way I could describe it. Sheer, naked horror.'

Teddy shook his head again. 'But
— was it an accident, then? What was the
medical opinion? The coroner's verdict?'

'Death by misadventure.'

Teddy gave a short laugh. 'I know
enough of English coroners to know what
that means!'

'Oh I know, indeed, but the circumstances . . . ' Francis broke off yet again.
'Look here, are you quite sure you want
to hear all of this?'

'Quite sure. As you said earlier, poor
Hamish has no family, and I'm his oldest
friend, pretty much. I couldn't get there
in time for the funeral — by the way your
letter, or one of them, said that it couldn't
be delayed — and that's another oddity.
But, since I couldn't, I'd like to find out
as much as possible about it all.'

Francis nodded. 'Fair enough. As to
the funeral, there was . . . well, it was
thought, I thought, *we* thought — the
firm I mean — it was best not to wait too
long.'

Teddy frowned. 'We'll let that pass, for
the time being. You were about to tell me

just how poor Hamish died?'

'He was found in a field,' said Francis, 'at a place called Docken Parva.'

'Aha!'

Francis leaned forward. 'You know it, then?'

'I know of it. That is, I know the name. Only what Hamish wrote to me about it. An old, deserted village, or something of the kind?'

'Something of the kind,' agreed Francis.

'Sorry, I interrupted you. The cause of death?'

Francis shrugged. 'I'm not a doctor, but the medical opinion was 'massive internal injuries' leading to death. Heart failure, I suppose — ultimately — in consequence of those injuries.'

'You say he was found in a field? Was there any animal, a bull or something, that might have gored him?'

Francis shook his head. 'I don't think I've made the thing quite clear, I'm afraid. There wasn't a mark on the body, unless you count that hideous expression I told you about. The injuries were to the various internal organs, but nothing

— nothing at all — to show how they'd occurred. No cuts or scars or any other sort of mark.'

'H'mm. Odd.'

'Indeed. As to a wild animal — or even a domestic animal run amok — there was no entrance to the field from the other fields round about which held farm stock, and no marks of any wild beast. Besides,' Francis added, 'this is rural England, not the wilds of America where you might expect to find a mountain lion! No, there was absolutely nothing to show how the injuries had been inflicted. Nothing whatever.' He hesitated. 'You don't know this area at all, I gather?'

Teddy shook his head.

'It's — well, it's a strange place, Docken, in many respects.'

'Look here, who was the doctor who looked at the body?'

'Dr Wilson, here in Snelling. Would you like an introduction to him?'

'Mr Lawrence? Sit down, please.'

Dr Wilson, like Mr Francis, was a young man, and Teddy — who again had half expected a much older man — felt his spirits rise. 'I'm a friend — '

'Yes, yes. Francis told me that you'd written to him, and that you were coming over to see us in person.' Dr Wilson paused, and took out a cigarette case. 'Do you?'

Teddy waved the offer aside. 'Doctor, I know that there are what you might call professional considerations which might make you reluctant to talk about a patient — a former patient — but I am, or was — rather — a very old and very good friend of poor Hamish's. That being the case — '

Dr Wilson held up a hand. 'My dear fellow! No need for all that, I assure you.' He hesitated, much as Francis had done earlier, and took his time over selecting and lighting a cigarette. 'No, the plain fact is that no professional consideration, as you term it, would count very strongly with me in this instance. However, there are other considerations which make it a rather painful topic to discuss. Neither you nor I, now, can do anything which might make any sort of difference to poor

McLean, so why rake over the thing? Just try to accept it as a tragic — '

'Accident?' The tone of Teddy's voice made his displeasure obvious.

Dr Wilson laughed sheepishly. 'Yes. Look here, you're a man of the world, I take it? Well, then, I'll tell you the difficulty. When we . . . when we looked at poor McLean's body, there wasn't any sign of an injury. None whatever. You understand that? Naturally there had to be a proper post-mortem examination, and that was the . . . the real devil of it, to be blunt.' He broke off for a moment. 'Look here, I don't normally drink during the day, but I think an exception might be justified in this case.' He stood up and went over to a locked cupboard, unlocked and opened it, and took out a bottle of whisky and two glasses. 'Will you join me?'

Teddy, feeling rather disappointed with the good doctor, said, 'Thanks, but I don't — '

'I would really recommend it. My professional advice, you know. No fee, of course.'

'In that case, perhaps a small one?' Better humour the fellow, thought Teddy. And a second thought followed hard on the heels of the first, to the effect that if this was the best the locality could provide by way of a medical man, then it was just as well that he had come here himself to look into the matter.

Dr Wilson handed Teddy a glass, and took a sip — no more — of his own before continuing. 'The only thing I've ever seen that was at all similar,' he said slowly, 'was an old tramp who must have had a good day's begging one market day, and taken a drop too much to drink, or more than a drop too much in fact. He must have stumbled in the road and the next thing anybody knew he was under the wheels of a hay wagon. Crushed his ribs, poor fellow, pushed them right into the chest, and the weight of the thing turned his lungs and other internal organs pretty much to pulp. Of course, in that instance, there were obvious external injuries to be seen.'

'I see. And Hamish — that was the kind of thing — ' Teddy took a drink, not a sip of his whisky, wishing now it had been a larger helping.

Dr Wilson nodded. 'Only with McLean, every organ — every single organ — in his body was in the same state. Pulp.' He, too, took a longer pull at his drink.

'Phew! I see. Yes, I do see. But . . . no external marks?'

Dr Wilson shook his head. 'Not a scratch on the body. Outside, at any rate.'

'But,' Teddy shook his head in disbelief, 'what could account for such a thing?'

'For the internal injuries? A fall, perhaps, from a very great height. Or a crushing injury, like the old fellow and the cart. But in either of those events there would be external marks as well. And there were none.'

'So. I mean to say, have you no conjecture — no guess — as to what might have done it?'

Dr Wilson shook his head. He leaned forward and lowered his voice, although the two men were alone in the consulting room. 'It looked — mind, this is not in any sense a medical opinion, rather a credulous man's fancy . . . It sounds sheer lunacy

— damn it, it *is* sheer lunacy! But it looked just as if someone — or something — had carefully removed his skin, beaten the insides to a pulp, and replaced the skin with equal care and consideration.' Teddy finished his whisky at a gulp. 'Another?'

'No, no thanks.' Teddy stood up, held out his hand. 'Look here, I know — well — I know that this must have been a bit awkward for you, Doctor. I can see, now, why you would have preferred not to discuss the matter. But I'm sure that, equally, you can see why I feel obliged to look into it further?'

'Oh, quite so. That is to say, I can and I can't. By which I mean — and I hope this doesn't sound patronising or anything — but you're a newcomer round here, and I'm not. All I can say is, if it were me, I'd leave well enough alone.'

Teddy looked closely at the doctor. 'Any particular reason for that advice?'

Dr Wilson shrugged his shoulders. 'Only that — well — there have been one or two odd occurrences round about here, in my time.'

'Odd. How *odd*?'

'I'd really prefer not to discuss it.'

Teddy stared at the other man. 'Oh, very well! But this is all very mysterious, I must say.' He felt this was perhaps a touch churlish, and added, 'Still, thank you for your time, and your frankness.'

'No trouble at all.'

'Oh,' said Teddy, who had just remembered something, 'that lawyer chap, Francis; he said he, or perhaps *you* — those involved, anyway — had thought it best not to delay Hamish's funeral. Was there any reason for that?'

'Not really. There were no relations to make a special journey, of course, so no reason to wait on that account. As for yourself, there was no telling whether you'd want to come, or how long it would take.'

It sounded plausible, but something — a hint of evasion, almost — in Dr Wilson's voice, made Teddy ask, 'And that was all?'

'There was . . . talk.' He gave an unconvincing laugh. 'They're a superstitious lot round here, I'm afraid.' He

42

glanced at his watch. 'If there was nothing more? Only I have my rounds to do, you know.'

There was, one need hardly remark, a good deal more, but Teddy could see quite clearly that further enquiry would be useless. He merely smiled, nodded, and shook hands before leaving.

* * *

A Doctorate in Divinity may, as the late Rev. Mr McLean had noted, be more appropriate to a bishop than to the rector of a fairly remote parish. And indeed the Rev. Hezekiah Hastings was — to all outward appearance — eminently suited more to an Episcopal palace than to a rundown rectory, being a man of some fifty years, and almost entirely bald, with a kindly — almost otherworldly — expression now rather marred by a worried frown.

Dr Hastings waved Teddy to a chair and produced a respectable sherry, for it was by now getting dark, though it was only around four o'clock in the afternoon.

'A trifle early,' he said without a hint of genuine apology in his voice, 'but I fear I have never got into the habit of afternoon tea, and one feels the need for a little refreshment at this hour.'

'Thank you, sir.' Teddy accepted his sherry, and sipped it cautiously.

'Now, you say you are — *were*, I suppose I ought to have said — a friend of Mr McLean's?'

'I was, sir. Perhaps his best friend.'

'And you are naturally anxious to find out just what happened to him?'

Teddy nodded. 'And I must say — if I may say so without giving offence, sir — that those to whom I have spoken already have been less than forthcoming on the subject.'

'Ah.' For a moment, Teddy thought that Dr Hastings was going to be similarly reticent, but after a short pause and another sip of sherry the older man went on. 'These professional men, so-called! Doctors and lawyers and the like — they won't commit themselves, my dear sir, and that's a fact! Frightened, I suppose. Frightened that people will talk, accuse them of being fanciful, over-imaginative, not quite rational. A clergyman, on the other hand — well, to a very great extent we deal in the unknown every day, we're used to thinking about things you can't see or hear, but just have to accept anyway. Take on faith, so to speak.'

Teddy was relieved. 'Yes. Of course you do, sir. That being so, I wondered if you might give me some hint as to what really happened to poor Hamish — Mr Mclean, that is?'

Dr Hastings coughed delicately, and studied his sherry glass carefully. 'I must say,' he began cautiously, 'the subject is — ah — a somewhat touchy one, and a somewhat painful one, despite my previous assertion as to my own suitability for consultation upon it.'

Teddy, feeling that an interruption might merely further postpone any discussion, said nothing.

Dr Hastings went on, 'Does the poet not say something to the effect that 'there are more things in heaven and earth' and so on. It's quite true, you know. It may, perhaps, already have occurred to you to wonder as to just why a place like Docken should have its own vicar? It is really so small that under normal circumstances there would be, at best, a curate. More likely there would be nobody at all and the church would serve merely as a chapel of ease, with the people ordinarily being obliged to come here on a Sunday should they wish to attend divine service.'

Teddy had lived in England long enough to know something of how things were done there. 'And you, yourself, sir,' he said, greatly daring, 'I did wonder . . . about . . . ' he found himself uncertain as to how to continue.

Dr Hastings seemed to catch Teddy's meaning, though, and gave a little smile of self-deprecation. 'You think that I am perhaps too highly qualified for the post of rector in such an out of the way spot? Well, sir, it is perhaps not for me to say it, but the plain fact is that for many years — possibly many centuries — it has been the custom to have a full-blown vicar at Docken, and to have an older, more experienced man here at Snelling.'

'And why is that, sir?'

Dr Hastings leaned forward. 'Because the history of the place — the occurrences, as it were, over the years, or the centuries — make it imperative that the church should have a presence here. Tell me, Mr Lawrence, do you believe in 'evil' as a concept?'

'I've known some very wicked men,' said Teddy. 'And, to be honest, some very wicked women as well. But 'evil' in the abstract? The devil walking abroad stinking of brimstone? With the greatest possible respect to your own views, sir, no, I don't really think I do.'

Dr Hastings nodded, as if that were what he had expected. 'No. You young chaps — all scientists and evolutionists I dare say — your modern theories have overshadowed the old teachings, of course. But I'm a bit more elderly, and I can tell you that some very strange things happen in this curious world of ours.' He sighed, 'And perhaps more particularly in this small corner of it. Naturally, it comes and goes,' he added, almost as an afterthought. Before Teddy could ask what he meant, he went on,

'Now, Mr McLean's predecessor, old Mr Farrer — I call him 'old'; he wasn't decrepit or anything, but he was twenty years my senior when he died — had knocked about a good bit. Done a lot of missionary work out in Africa, where the folk are not quite as sophisticated as ourselves — rough diamonds, you know — are not quite so eager to scoff at things which they don't understand.'

Teddy waited a moment, then said. 'You will, I'm sure, forgive me, Dr Hastings, but there is a great deal about all this that I don't understand. I'm sure that all you've said is quite true, but you still have not said just what you think happened to Hamish.'

'Ah.' Dr Hastings studied his sherry glass again. 'No, indeed. And of course you — indeed you are fully entitled to — yes.' He looked round his study, although it contained only the two of them, but this was something to which Teddy was by now pretty much becoming accustomed, lowered his voice to a conspiratorial whisper, and said: 'Witch-craft!'

'Witchcraft?' Teddy, who had unconsciously leaned forward in sympathy, sank back into his chair, and his voice showed the disappointment he felt.

Dr Hastings shrugged his shoulders. 'You see? You ask my opinion, and reject it out of hand once given!' He gazed at Teddy with the benevolent smile of a father considering a mildly errant son. 'Nevertheless, that's my private opinion, for what it is worth.'

Frankly, thought Teddy, it wasn't worth much at all. It did, however, explain why a man with Dr Hastings' qualifications should end his days in a rural rectory. Clearly the bishop had got wind of Hastings' odd beliefs and put him out to pasture, sent him where he could do little or no harm. Teddy smiled back, as genuinely as he could manage.

Dr Hastings' smile broadened. 'Humour the poor old chap, is that it?'

'No, no! But — well . . . '

'I understand, my boy, believe me, I well understand. Your reaction is precisely the same as my own when old Bishop

Beaumont — dead now, of course — asked me to 'volunteer', as he put it, to serve out here.' The smile vanished and sighed again, more deeply. 'Well, I've changed my mind since those days, I can tell you.'

'You must admit, sir — '

'Oh, I do! Have you not been out to Docken yet?' Teddy shook his head. 'No. If you do — mind, I wouldn't advise it — you'll see for yourself that it's a very . . . odd sort of place, I suppose I should say. Yes, distinctly odd. The people,' he glanced round and lowered his voice again, 'don't travel much outside the village and so — well, frankly, 'inbreeding' would be the modern term, although I'm afraid that we called it by a somewhat ruder name at theological college. Yes, very strange people, although one tries not to judge.' He stood up suddenly. 'No good talking to you youngsters! Have you dined, by the way?'

Teddy, appreciably thrown by Dr Hastings' revelation, realised that in fact he had not eaten all day, but had drunk a small whisky and a large sherry, and was

50

both hungry and light-headed in consequence. 'No, sir, I seem to have been so
busy the thought never occurred to me.'

'Then you'll dine here. No argument!
My wife is dead, of course, but my
daughter keeps house very well for me,
and we have an excellent cook. I'll ring to
make sure there's enough, though I have
no doubt.' Before Teddy could say
anything else, Dr Hastings had rung the
bell and given instructions to the maid
who appeared in answer to it. When the
matter was settled, he asked Teddy, 'And
where are you staying tonight?'

'Again, I have not really — '

'Then you can stay here, at the
Rectory. No argument there either! We
have plenty of spare bedrooms, and
there's only one inn with rooms to let at
Snelling — which is not even suitable for
the farmers and commercial travellers
who patronise it. No, my dear fellow,
you'll stay here tonight, for you'll not get
back to Dunchester for your train — not
now.'

'My train, sir?'

'Back to London.' Dr Hastings beheld

Teddy, 'I take it you will be going back as soon as may be?'

'No, sir, I plan to say here — in Docken Magna, that is to say — for a week or so, to look into Hamish's death.' Until the words were said, Teddy had not known what in fact his intentions were. He had come to England without thinking — almost instinctively — and now, just as instinctively, he saw what he must do.

'Oh, dear!' Dr Hastings appeared quite distressed at this news. 'The village — well, there is not even a rudimentary inn such as we have here, only a beer-house, without rooms and meals and hot water! If you are determined to stay in the area for a few days, I suppose we could put you up here, although it is a substantial walk into Docken — unless you hire a cart or trap, or some such.'

'That's very kind of you, sir,' said Teddy, with conviction, 'but I think I should prefer — is there nowhere in Docken, no cottage, however, humble, that would find me a bed and a simple meal?'

Dr Hastings shook his head. 'The people are not exactly welcoming to strangers.' He stared doubtfully at Teddy, as if seeing him for the first time. 'If you are set on staying in the village, then we might do worse than give you a key to the vicarage. I have a spare here.'

'Why thank you, sir!'

'Mind you, I wouldn't recommend it. For one thing, the place will be damp. It's been empty these past few weeks, and at this time of year . . . ' The days had been cold, and the sky gave promise of snow, though none had fallen lately. 'No servants in the place, of course,' Dr Hastings continued, 'although Mrs Oldman did go in every day to keep the house tidy and cook a meal for poor McLean.'

'That sounds admirable.'

'I don't know about that.' Dr Hastings did not agree. 'Do you have any luggage?'

'I travel light, sir.' Teddy nodded towards a large holdall which he had brought with him, having hauled it around all day, and left in a corner of the study.

'A man after my own heart; can't do

with a load of traps and steamer trunks. Well then, tomorrow we shall arrange a ride for you with the grocer's cart. It goes into Docken three times a week, to keep them supplied.'

★   ★   ★

'Bound for Docken, mister?' The grocer's assistant and carter, a generally uncommunicative man, spoke as if Docken Magna were at the end of the earth; as if he, personally, had neither been there nor desired to, and Teddy was headed for a destination unknown.

'Yes.' Two can be uncommunicative, thought Teddy. He was in tolerably good spirits, Dr Hastings having given him a satisfying dinner last night and a hearty breakfast this morning. Teddy had met Miss Hastings, and found her rather ordinary and a touch silly. So, the grocer's man having refused all offers of help when unloading goods in and around Little Snelling and smaller places on the way — and having broken an hour's silence to ask this asinine question

— Teddy was pleased to answer him in kind.

'Bound for the vicarage?'

'Indeed.'

'Aye.' A short pause, then, 'Stranger in these parts?'

'My first visit.' Teddy wondered if he couldn't perhaps extract some information from such a humble source, having acquired little enough from those he had thus far consulted. 'I am — or was — a friend of the late vicar, Mr McLean.'

'Aye?' The man shook his head grimly. 'A bad business, that, mister.'

'Aye?' It was said before Teddy could help it, but seemed to cause no offence.

'Aye. And I'll tell you this, mister, were I you — vicarage or no vicarage — I'd lock my door of a night. And my windows into the bargain.'

'Oh? I shouldn't have thought an out of the way place like this would be much troubled by anything more wicked than the occasional bit of poaching.'

'Wicked?' The grocer's man turned this over in his mind in silence for a moment, then hawked and spat into the ditch.

'Don't know as to that, mister, but were I you, I'd lock my doors of a night.' He gestured with his whip to where the road curved out of sight behind a thorn hedge, its dark branches now lightly dusted with the snow that was just beginning to fall. 'Docken round the next bend.'

The cart lumbered round the sharp turn in the lane, and Teddy was somewhat disappointed to see nothing more than a ramshackle cottage on the right hand side, another on the left some hundred yards further on, and then another bend in the road. 'Not a big place, is it?'

'Nay. Mind, this isn't what you'd call Docken proper. Main of the place is round this next bend.'

Teddy was prepared this time, and thus neither surprised nor disappointed to see that the 'main of the place' consisted of half a dozen cottages every bit as dilapidated as those he had seen already, scattered down a furlong of fairly straight road. 'Is this all there is?'

'Aye. And more than enough, did you ask me.'

'What do the people do?' Teddy wanted to know.

'Do?' The grocer's man was evidently puzzled.

'You know: do they work on farms, or knit stockings at home, or just what?'

The man pushed back his cap and scratched his head. 'Some do work for Farmer Burton,' he conceded, 'but mostly his folk live at the farm, or the little cottages round about it.'

'Where is that?'

'Burton's Farm, they call it.'

Teddy sighed.

'Oh, aye, I see. Out by what you'd call Docken Parva,' the man pointed with his whip as he elaborated. 'A short mile away, the farm. As for t' other folk, they — well, I don't rightly know what they do.' He scratched his head again, as if to inspire thought. 'Squire Partridge, I suppose he looks after them, like.'

'Yes, Mr Partridge. He's the biggest landowner hereabouts, I believe? I meant to ask you where he lives.'

The grocer's man brought his cart to a standstill, and pointed again. 'See that little lane, just before that last cottage? Go up there, no more than two — maybe three — minutes, you'll find his old place. Now, you're bound for the vicarage, did you say? See the lane off t' other side of the road, halfway down? Vicarage and church, they're both five minutes up that way.'

'Thank you. What about a Mr and Mrs Oldman, where might I find them?'

'Cottage just before the church lane. I'll take you there and up to the vicarage before I unload Widow Granger's goods.'

'No need for that, thanks very much,' said Teddy. 'Thanks to you, I can find my way well enough now, and I'd like to speak to Mrs Oldman and Mr Partridge before I go to the vicarage.'

'Suit yourself. I'll be here a while, anyway. I take a bite of bread and cheese at the Crooked Billet before I set off back, a dreary old day like this. If so happens you need me, you know where to find me.'

'Yes, thanks again.' Teddy produced a small silver coin, which much to his surprise was waved away.

'No need for that,' mumbled the grocer's man. 'Just doing my job.'

'Go on,' urged Teddy. 'Have a glass of beer on me, with your bread and cheese?'

'Well, then,' said the man, as if the notion were new to him. 'I won't throw your kindness in your face, mister, and thanks.' He jerked his head at the nearest cottage, 'Widow Granger's. Nearest thing to a shop in the place, should you need aught. If she hasn't got it, she'll order it from town next time I call.'

Teddy nodded, climbed down from the cart, and retrieved his trusty holdall. 'Thanks again,' he said, setting off in the direction of the Oldman cottage. As he did so, a woman — presumably Mrs Granger — came out of the cottage that served for the village shop. She stared at Teddy without any sort of curiosity and ignored him when he wished her a good morning. Odd indeed, he reflected, but thought no more of it as he strode the few score yards to the Oldman door, and knocked loudly.

It was opened by a woman apparently

identical to Mrs Granger — so much so that Teddy actually looked back over his shoulder to where the grocer's man was unloading the cart. 'Oh — I beg your pardon. Mrs Oldman?'

This knotty problem was weighed in silence for a few moments. 'I am.'

'My name is Lawrence, and I'm staying at the vicarage.'

Once again Mrs Oldman thought about this a while. 'No good you going to the vicarage, there's nobody up there now.'

After several more minor misunderstandings Teddy managed to secure Mrs Oldman's services to the extent that she would light a fire or two at the vicarage, set fresh linen on the bed, and prepare a meal for the evening.

'Mind,' she added, 'it'll only be cold pie, but there's a bottle of something or other in the cupboard — or should be. Not that Vicar was a drinking man,' she added rather hastily, making Teddy — who had not known McLean as an abstainer in his youth — wonder if Mr Oldman had not informally acquired some of the late vicar's cellar.

However, he was so pleased at having successfully concluded his arrangements, that he let this pass, merely saying that he wanted to see Mr Partridge, and would return to the vicarage as soon as may be. Teddy enquired if Mr Oldman might be home, as he would have liked a word with him, but apparently the man of the house was 'over to Burton's farm', at present. 'Have you a key?' asked Mrs Oldman. Teddy produced the key given to him by Dr Hastings. 'Well, that's all right, then. See, I've a key myself, but did I give you that, I couldn't get in, could I?'

'No, indeed not.' Their domestic arrangements were going to be positively scintillating, thought Teddy. 'Thank you so much, Mrs Oldman, I'm sure I'll see you later.'

'Not if it's dark, you won't. Folk round here don't like to be out after dark.'

'Oh.'

★   ★   ★

Mr Partridge's house, which Teddy found easily enough, was a good deal more substantial than the rundown cottages in the village street. It was, in fact, as typical a manor house as one might expect, set in among trees and fronted by a garden that was both formally laid out and decidedly untidy. When Teddy was admitted by an elderly manservant, he saw there was even a great hall inside the door, presumably a relic of some medieval establishment.

Mr Partridge came bustling out to greet his visitor. The squire was a man of indeterminate age — fifty or sixty — and was not unlike Teddy's private image of Mr Pickwick, being inclined to baldness and a slight fussiness of manner, and wearing a pair of wire-rimmed spectacles which he looked over rather than through. 'Mr Lawrence, is it? From America, I understand? Yes, indeed, we have heard of you, sir, and half expected you, as well. A sad business, sir, a very sad business.' Mr Partridge gestured at the holdall which, since it was not particularly heavy, Teddy hadn't thought to leave anywhere. 'Got your kit, have you? Good, that means you can stay here tonight, or for as long as you wish.'

'That's very kind of you, sir,' said Teddy, 'but I've rather arranged to stay at the vicarage for a few days.'

'Ah! The vicarage? I see.' Mr Partridge digested this. Evidently, swift replies were not highly regarded hereabouts. 'Well,' he went on at last, 'I suppose your mind is made up. Though if you should change it at any time, just let me know, and we'll find a bed here for you. You're probably hungry, I imagine? It's a fair way from Snelling, and the weather has taken a turn for the worse today, I fear. I dine in the middle of the day at this time of year, and would be delighted if you'd join me. We'll have a long talk — I know there must be many questions you wish to ask and I'll do my very best to answer them — then I'll take you over to the vicarage before it gets too dark to see the way. No street lamps here, you know!'

Teddy, upon whom twelve miles of crisp, late January air had produced a keen appetite, thanked him profusely. Mr Partridge apologised for the fact that it was only a few minutes past noon, and produced a bottle of excellent sherry, followed soon after by a roast fowl complete with trimmings.

'My housekeeper, Mrs King, looks after me very well,' said Mr Partridge. 'Of course,' he added thoughtfully, 'she isn't from these parts.'

Teddy thought it best not to enquire as to just what his host meant by that, asking instead, 'Earlier on, sir, you seemed to think that my staying at the vicarage wasn't such a good idea. Was there a reason for that?'

'Only that the old place will be damp, and such, you know.'

'Mrs Oldman has promised to air it, and light fires.'

'Ah, yes. She's a good woman, not — perhaps — too intelligent, but a good heart.'

'She bears a strong resemblance to Mrs Granger, are they sisters — or otherwise related?'

'A small place like this — you know,' Mr Partridge smiled as one man of the world to another. 'If the truth be told, I dare say I'm a distant cousin of more than half the people here.'

'And feel responsible for them accordingly? There cannot be too much in the way of work, round about?'

'There are one or two farms, of course, but yes, one does feel a certain *noblesse oblige*, and such. As I was saying, Mrs Oldman will at least make the vicarage habitable for you. It'll need it, what with the damp.'

'Just damp? It isn't — ' Teddy hesitated, then thought that he might just as well try and get some sensible opinions on what was troubling him. 'The vicarage isn't haunted, or anything, is it? Reputed to be, I should say, because I imagine you're as sceptical as I am about these primitive beliefs.'

'Haunted? Dear me, no. The church, of course . . . ' Mr Partridge trailed off.

'The church?'

'I was going to say that the Church rather pooh-poohs that sort of thing,' he replied vaguely. Teddy had the distinct impression that the squire had not originally intended to say anything of the kind. Mr Partridge proceeded immediately, 'As for being a sceptic, I can understand your views, but I'm afraid that having lived here all my life, I am reluctant to condemn these old beliefs — superstitions you might call them — too strongly.'

Teddy nodded, embarrassed not for the first time in the last day or so. Emboldened by the sherry, or the fine wine Mr Partridge had served with the meal, he asked, 'I have tried to determine exactly what happened to poor Hamish — McLean, that is — but all I get is a lot of . . . well, nonsense. You can't tell me anything, can you?'

Mr Partridge coughed delicately, and Teddy was not encouraged by the sound. 'It depends very much, you know, on just what one is prepared to believe. Things have changed a good deal in the world even in my time. Electricity, motor cars — I dare say you have a motor car back home?'

'I don't, but my father does. Not very reliable,' Teddy laughed.

'But you take my meaning? A century

ago, who would ever have thought candles would be replaced by a simple switch, or horses by evil-smelling engines? Belief, even the various shades of Christianity . . . a funny thing, belief.'

'Yes, indeed, but what about Hamish? What do your beliefs say about him?'

'Ah.' Mr Partridge looked over his spectacles at Teddy. 'Mr McLean. You see, as I say, we — my family, I mean — have been here for a good time now, and in that time we have seen a good many queer things happen in the place.' Before Teddy could put the obvious question, Mr Partridge raised a hand, and went on, 'What sort of queer things? Well, unexplained deaths, such as that of your unfortunate friend. Oh, not as what you might call a regular occurrence, but sufficient in number — counted over the years — to make one wonder if the old tales might not be true after all.'

'What might those old tales be, sir?' asked Teddy. 'People seem to be reticent about them, unless perhaps they just don't know. But even the most unimaginative men — the fellow from the grocer's

67

shop in Great Snelling, for instance — seem to feel as if something is amiss here. He went so far as to give me this.' Teddy produced the little wood carving the grocer's man had given him, and passed it to Mr Partridge.

'Dear me!' said Mr Partridge as he examined it closely. 'I've seen such objects before. A charm, I suppose you'd call it, or a *ju-ju* as they might say in Africa. As to its efficacy, real or imagined . . . ' He gave a weary smile which spoke volumes, and handed the charm back. 'But you do see how the place has a reputation far — relatively far — afield?'

'Is that on the basis of these unexplained deaths? I would have thought that if they are indeed occasional, their occurrence would not be so remarkable as to produce the reputation you speak of, especially in an out of the way village such as this.'

'Indeed not. We are a long way from doctors and surgeons and the panoply of the dissecting room! As you suggest, country folk tend to make a mystery where none exists — but there is the entire history of the place to be considered, too.'

'Is there?' This, thought Teddy, was more like it.

'Did McLean not tell you any of it?'

'The truth, sir, is that Hamish had scarcely time to settle in to his new duties before his death. All I know is that he took an interest in local customs and legends.'

'I see. He did not pass anything he had learned on to you? No? Well, let me see,' Mr Partridge refilled his glass, and offered the bottle to Teddy, who refused. 'At one time the village was a mile or so down the road, at what is now known as Docken Parva. I see you have heard the name. The folk there had the reputation of serving old gods — '

'Pagans, you mean? Woden, Thor, and the like?'

'No, much earlier than that, I imagine. The Romans — we have Roman remains here, you know — pretty much suppressed the old ways, moved the village here, and left only a farmstead where the previous settlement had been. Hence the

69

'Magna' and 'Parva' nomenclature. By the time the Saxon pagans arrived, the old ways had re-emerged, and were again suppressed. This was followed by the witch-fever of the medieval days, of course. Many a savage deed was done in this old place.' He shook his head sadly and took a sip of his wine.

'You will forgive me, sir, but surely this talk of Romans and Saxons and witches is ancient history, in the most literal sense?'

'Ah,' Mr Partridge had the grace to blush slightly. 'Family records, you know, speak of the witch trials, so that much is certain. As to the rest, amateur archaeology has been pretty much a mania with my people over the years. True, I suppose much of what I have told you is speculation, but speculation based upon sound evidence, sir!' Teddy was nonplussed, but Mr Partridge saved him from the need to provide an appropriate response by looking at the clock. 'Our conversation has been so interesting that I'd not realised it was so late. It will be dark soon, and I promised to show you the way to the vicarage.'

'Please don't trouble yourself, sir. I can find my way quite easily.'

'No trouble at all. I see that it's starting to snow, so it might be as well if I accompany you.' Mr Partridge stubbornly refused to be put off. He walked with Teddy back through the village street, and up the lane on the far side, stopping outside a very ugly house built in the early Victorian style. 'The old vicarage was burnt down,' he explained. 'I have often deplored the economies which dictated this rather repellent architecture, but what is the use?' He watched as Teddy unlocked the door, and added, 'There is electricity laid on. Ah, you've found the switch! Makes the old place seem quite cheerful, does it not?'

'Will you step in a moment, sir? I don't know what there is in the way of refreshment, but — '

'No, thank you. I must be getting back, and you'll need to make yourself comfortable in the place. Perhaps once you've settled in, you will feel inclined to repeat the invitation, and I to accept it.' Mr Partridge shook hands and raised his antiquated hat in farewell. After a couple of paces he turned round. 'Mind, should you decide — for any reason — that the vicarage is not to your taste, then the offer of a bed at my house still stands. Any time, you know.'

And off he went.

★ ★ ★

Teddy woke early next morning, perhaps the natural consequence of sleeping in a strange bed. He had found his way about the house without the slightest difficulty, including the cold pie left by Mrs Oldman. It was quite delicious and Teddy had muttered some nonsense to the effect that it contained some of Mr Partridge's partridges. Together with the half bottle of Long John scotch whisky he found in a cupboard, and the pipe and decent tobacco he'd bought in London, Teddy had done himself well the previous evening and turned in early. Mrs Oldman had thoughtfully put a stone hot water bottle in the bed, so he'd dropped off to sleep at once. Perhaps he had turned in a bit too early. That might explain his waking at an hour which, if not actually ungodly, was a touch less than heavenly. Still, it did mean he could turn over for a few minutes — or more — and that was no privation, for the air outside the blankets felt chilly, as if there had been a hard frost.

Teddy eventually, reluctantly, rose from his bed, dressed, and made his way downstairs to the kitchen. There was an old-fashioned range with an oven and the like, upon which stood a kettle of water. The fire had burned low overnight, but a shovelful of coals procured a cheerful blaze, and in a few minutes the water in the kettle was hot enough for a wash, a shave, and a blessed cup of tea.

Teddy's preparations were interrupted by Mrs Oldman letting herself in at the kitchen door. She looked askance at Teddy fiddling with the stove, made reference to 'the damper', and proceeded to arrange the mysterious device to her own satisfaction before allowing him to take his hot water upstairs.

By the time Teddy returned to the

kitchen, feeling considerably more blithe, Mrs Oldman had prepared his breakfast of eggs and bacon, and made a very good job of it too. As he ate, she asked, 'You wanted to see Oldman, sir?'

'Is your husband at home?'

Mrs Oldman looked at him, and he noticed her eyes had a peculiar blankness. 'He's at home, now. If so you'd care to step down to the house, you'll find him at home. Meantime,' she added with a disparaging glance around, and an audible sniff, 'I'd best take a duster to the place. And if so you do go out, mind your step, for it's slippy underfoot.'

Teddy finished his meal and then, well wrapped up and shod in stout boots, ventured outside with his pipe. He blew a great cloud of smoke into the clear, frosty air, and set off. The lane was icy, but a couple of villagers were out and about. Although they ignored his greetings, Teddy noticed that they looked a touch 'vacant', with the same blank eyes. This was not the only respect in which they resembled Mrs Oldman and Mrs Granger, for they all bore very similar features.

Really, this was inbreeding with a vengeance. Teddy had heard of 'the village idiot', but here was a village well on its way to being entirely populated by imbeciles.

A few minutes' walk brought him to the Oldman cottage, and he knocked at the door. It was opened by a perfectly ordinary looking man — Teddy noted with relief that his features were distinct from the other villagers — dressed in shabby clothes. 'Mr Oldman?'

'Aye. You'll be Mr Lawrence, I reckon? Come in, sir.'

There followed the usual pleasantries. Teddy offered Mr Oldman a fill of tobacco, which was accepted, and then got down to business. 'Mr Oldman, I'm really here to find out how Mr McLean died. Nobody seems able — or willing — to tell me, and I wondered if you might know anything about it? I'd be most grateful, just for my own peace of mind.'

'Peace of mind?' For a moment, Teddy could have sworn Mr Oldman sounded amused at this, but the other man appeared quite serious as he adjusted the filling of his pipe, and Teddy assumed he was mistaken. 'I'll tell you this: he died in a thunderstorm.'

'Oh. Do you get thunder at this time of year . . . Are you saying he was struck by lightning, or something like that? Because in that case — '

'Lightning?' Mr Oldman did not trouble to hide his contempt. 'He wasn't struck by no lightning! No, what I'm telling you is this, mister: whenever *They* come, it's always in a thunderstorm.'

'*They?*'

Mr Oldman nodded. 'Or *Him*, as may be. Some folk say one thing, some another.'

Teddy shook his head. 'I don't follow you, I'm afraid. Is this another of the local legends, or — '

'No legend, mister. You'll have seen that — *thing?*' Mr Oldman's speech was littered with curious emphases, which Teddy thought of as Capital Letter Mania.

'I'm sorry, I don't — '

'In the churchyard?' Mr Oldman gazed at a garishly sentimental calendar advertising a popular brand of cocoa. 'Today's

Saturday, isn't it? Well, you just keep an eye on the church tomorrow. You'll see.' He nodded mysteriously.

Somehow Mr Oldman managed to deflect all the supplementary questions which Teddy put to him. Frustrated, Teddy took his leave after a few minutes more of pointless conversation, returning the way he'd come. This time he turned right instead of left at the top of the lane, thereby came to the church rather than the vicarage.

The church was a much older building than the vicarage. Norman, perhaps. Certainly the entrance porch had the arched top and heavy oaken door which spoke of Duke William and his contemporaries. There seemed nothing special about the edifice, though possible the interior might repay the attention of the ecclesiologist. Teddy glanced inside, which seemed — as is so often the way with rural churches — to be far too large for the needs of the current population. There was, however, nothing to interest a man who was not a specialist in church furnishings or architecture, and Teddy stood there irresolute. He was for a moment at something of a loss as to what to do with the rest of the day. Had he wasted his time, and a considerable amount of money, travelling here from Boston? It was looking that way. More irritating than any waste of time and money was the insidious thought that he was making himself look just a little foolish.

He turned to go, but — as he closed the heavy door behind him — it struck him that he might spend a few minutes looking for the curious statue or figure McLean had noted. It was, Teddy recalled, somewhere in the churchyard, and it must be fairly obvious to the casual observer. He wandered slowly down the path, noting the broken-down tomb-stones, on a few of which he could just make out worn inscriptions: 'Jabez Oldman' and 'Elizabeth . . . , Gone to The Lord, AD 157 . . . ' There seemed to be many Oldmans resting here, but strangely enough the name 'Partridge' appeared to be absent. Teddy lifted his eyes from the gravestones and looked round, seeing a small but substantially-built stone structure at the side of the church. Some sort of mausoleum for the squirearchy? He went over to it. It was evidently a tomb for it had the usual cross over the door — no, there was a cross alright, but it consisted of two bones carved at right angles and surmounted by a skull, though this was much worn and not easy to spot. A macabre conceit, but quite typical of the sixteenth or seventeenth century, when the thing had very likely been built. There was no family name on the building, but there appeared to have been a coat of arms or something similar which had at some time been rather brutally defaced with a chisel. He rattled the door handle, and found it securely locked.

Teddy returned to the path. He went down as far as the gate by which he had originally entered the churchyard without seeing anything remotely resembling a statue. Disappointed, he looked around again, and noticed another entrance to the churchyard over towards the vicarage side. A lych-gate, with the usual little porch affair over it, gave onto the narrow path by which coffins were brought in for burials. Despite his robust scepticism and the warm clothes he wore, Teddy could not repress a slight shiver. He nevertheless went over to the lych-gate and looked inside the stone porch round it.

There, sitting on a ledge just inside the gate, was a small stone carving, for all the world like some heathen idol. About nine or ten inches high, no more, and not of the local stone, which was a brownish granite Teddy had never seen before. This carving was soapstone, unless Teddy was very much mistaken, but he would not have expected to find soapstone around these parts. And McLean had been right, the thing did seem all arms and legs. Or perhaps it was hair. Now that Teddy examined it closely, its face was weather-worn and flattened, with no features discernible, although the hair seemed to hang down in long locks. He wasn't sure if 'locks' was the correct word, but the hair was a long tangle, at any rate, and seemed to merge with the lower limbs in an odd way that reminded Teddy of something. He couldn't be sure if it was Medusa, the Green Man, or Mithras. There was an inscription carved on the base of the statue, but — like the face — it was too worn to be made out properly. Giving regard to McLean's opinion, Teddy supposed it might read 'shaggai' or 'S Haggai'. But then it might equally read 'shaggy' — accurate enough if it referred to the hairstyle — or 'thuggee', or 'A Present From Southend', or indeed just about anything one cared to read into it. There were a few withered flowers scattered around the base of the thing and something else — mouldy bread, perhaps — like some rude votive offering.

Intrigued, Teddy reached out to pick it up for a closer look — then jumped as someone shouted, 'Don't!' He turned, and was considerably surprised to see Mr Oldman standing a few feet away. Oldman must have followed him to the church, Teddy realised, now recovered from his surprise and slightly annoyed. He was about to make a remark, when Oldman added, 'You didn't touch that

— that *thing*, did you?'

'Why, no.'

Oldman nodded sagely. 'Best you didn't, mister. T'other chap — vicar, as was — he messed about with it, and you know what happened to him.'

'In a thunderstorm?' Teddy couldn't help himself.

Oldman shook his head. 'Some folk won't be told. I've tried. At least I can say that to anybody.'

He seemed sincere and Teddy felt ashamed at making fun of a man who had, after all, had none of his own advantages in life. He said, quickly, 'Look here, Mr Oldman, I'm very sorry if I sounded flippant and if I seem to be taking your words and warnings too lightly. But you must see that to me — as an outsider, a stranger here — it all seems very far-fetched!'

Oldman, who had half-turned to leave, appeared mollified. 'Aye, that's likely enough true. You see, mister, my family's been here for a lot of years and we've kind of grown used to the goings-on. Take it for granted, like.'

'I see that, but you must appreciate that it's very annoying that nobody will tell me just what these *goings-on* are? Unexplained deaths, I gather, but — '

'And the rest,' Oldman interrupted.

'Oh?'

Oldman looked around furtively — actually looked all the way around, which took Teddy slightly aback — and lowered his voice. 'You'll have seen one or two of the folk hereabouts? All look alike, pretty much, don't they? Even the wife,' he added with a touch of sadness.

'I assumed . . . a small place like this — marriage within the village, and so on . . . '

'There's that, I'll allow. But there's more to it than that. Things a man doesn't like to talk about, or even to own to himself.' Teddy could do nothing but sigh. 'Well, I'll tell you, even if you don't believe me — and you won't, I know that! There's *things* hereabouts, unholy *things, things* not of this world. Aye, laugh! But it's true enough, and you'll find out for yourself if you stay here long enough.'

He seemed offended, so Teddy said

hastily, 'Again, I'm sorry if I find it hard to accept, but please go on.'

'Nothing much more to tell. *They* — whoever, or whatever — *they* maybe come here in . . . ' he hesitated, looking for the right words.

'A thunderstorm?' suggested Teddy. This time there was no levity in his voice.

'Aye, you might call it that. Come to think, I couldn't tell you another word for it. Only it isn't like a proper thunderstorm, if you follow me? A lot of lightning, the odd rattle of thunder, but not like any thunderstorm you ever saw.'

'Just the lightning, electrical disturbances?' Teddy was intrigued.

'Aye,' Oldman nodded. 'And that's when they come. *They* — *they* do pretty much what they want . . . and then — and then go back . . . to wherever *they* come from.'

'And since *they* — whoever they are — have their way with the village maidens — sorry, I'm not trying to be funny, just to put it delicately — that's why all the folk here look alike?'

Oldman nodded. 'That's it.'

'But *you* don't. And Mr Partridge doesn't. How do you explain that?'

Oldman shook his head. 'Can't. Look, mister, I may not be able to explain things very well — and I certainly can't explain everything — but I'm doing my best. There just aren't words to tell a lot of what I've seen.'

'Yes, I understand that, but do try. What about these strange deaths, for instance? Are *they* responsible for those? And if so, why?' Oldman looked down and muttered something incomprehensible. 'What was that?'

'A lot of 'em's strangers, like your friend the vicar. Don't know what to expect, don't know how to keep safe — or as safe as you can be. And then I think that sometimes *they* kill as you or I might kill a cow or a sheep.'

'What, for food?'

'Aye, or for fun — like the gentry kill a fox or a fish they aren't going to eat.'

'Good Lord!'

'Not that He's a lot of use,' said Oldman with grim humour.

'At any rate, you've been more

straightforward than anyone with whom I've yet spoken.' Even, he thought to himself, if you've just told me the biggest load of gibberish since Munchausen. There was no doubt of that. Thunderstorms that weren't thunderstorms, but which allowed evil spirits or creatures from another world to come and disport themselves in — of all places on God's good earth — Docken Parva! Oldman, with his purely local reputation as a healer, or whatever he pretended to be, probably used spells and incantations along with his herbs and potions, and believed the nonsense he chanted over his cauldron.

But what about Hamish?

Looking at it logically, suppose Hamish had been found in — say, London — with massive internal injuries. Would the obvious conclusion not have been that there was foul play? Poor old Hamish had very likely broken — without realising it — some local taboo, and one of these inbred idiots had done him to death. The absence of external marks, of course, was a puzzle, but then perhaps Hamish had been beaten with a sack of flour or grain or some bucolic weapon that left no cuts or bruises. The bruises may have appeared after death, but the body had been hastily — and was that haste itself not suspicious — buried. The 'examination', if the word was even appropriate, had been by a doctor who hit the bottle in the middle of the day, but even the incompetent medico of Great Snelling might have found obvious signs of injury were it not for the unseemly rush to inter the corpse. Triumphant, Teddy returned his attention to Oldman, who was regarding the statue in silence.

'Do *they* look like this thing, then?'

'I couldn't say.'

'Oh?'

Oldman shook his head again. 'It's very funny, but you never remember seeing *them*.'

'H'mm.'

'And another thing — the time's all wrong.'

'I don't follow.'

'Well, how can I explain it? You see, you get this — lightning, I'll call it — lightning, and then next thing you know it'll be few hours after.'

Teddy frowned. 'After what?'

'After it should be, by rights. Say the lightning stuff comes in the morning. Then it seems as if it's only been a few minutes, see, but you'll find it's late afternoon.'

'A whole chunk of time missing, is that right? Like waking up after a heavy night and being unable to remember just where you were, or how much you had to drink?'

Oldman nodded. 'I see you're laughing at me again, but aye, that's just it.'

I'll bet it is, thought Teddy, wondering what Oldman put in his potions. 'I still don't see why this figure is here, in the churchyard, if it represents evil, as you seem to think.'

Oldman shrugged, indifferent to Teddy's logic. 'Couldn't rightly say. I do know, or at any rate I have the feeling, that they gather round it. Anyway, it's always been there, to keep the *evil* — as you yourself called it — outside the church.'

'But what if it acts as a ... a *magnet* ... for these *things*. Then surely it would be better moved right away from the village? Or destroyed completely?'

Oldman smiled. 'Destroy it? I wouldn't, not if I was you, mister. And as for moving it — well, then you'd never know just where *they* might turn up, would you now?'

'No, I suppose not.'

Oldman turned to leave. 'Just you keep watch tomorrow. Look out of the vicarage window. You'll see.'

As he watched Oldman walk down the lane back to the village, Teddy realised just how isolated the place was. He had the rest of the day before him and absolutely no idea as to how to occupy himself. He was thus considerably heartened to see Mrs Oldman emerge from the vicarage door and wave at him.

He walked quickly down the path and called out, 'Are you off, Mrs Oldman?'

'I'm off now. I've tidied the place as best I can, and I've left your tea in the oven. It's only lamb stew, but it'll be ready by tea-time. And there's bread and cheese for your dinner, if you want it. I'll look in again tomorrow.' At which she left without waiting to hear the thanks Teddy had to call after her.

He entered the vicarage by the kitchen door and was further cheered by the aroma which greeted him. Judging by the cold pie last night, Mrs Oldman — though she might be neither attractive nor intelligent — was a very good cook. Whatever else might happen to him, Teddy wouldn't starve to death. He had a slice of bread and small piece of cheese, then decided to walk to the famous Docken Parva, to see if he could find anything of interest there. He wrapped up once more in coat and scarf, and set out along the lane to the village, turning right at the Oldman cottage as indicated by the grocer's man. Ten minutes along the narrow road, its surface now turned to iron by the cold, Teddy saw a farmstead on his left.

There was an elderly man working in

the yard, and Teddy hailed him cheerfully. 'Mr Burton?'

'Aye?'

'My name's Lawrence, I'm — I was, that is — a friend of the late vicar, Mr McLean.'

'Aye.' The farmer took off his cap, respectfully. 'A bad business that, sir. Won't you step in, have some dinner?'

'Thank you, no, I've just had something to eat. What I would like to do is to see the field where Mr McLean was found.'

Mr Burton's brows knitted, but he pointed the way readily enough. 'Across this field here, over the lane — you'll see it. There's a locked gate, never been undone in all my time here, so you'll have to climb over should you want to go in. Mind, I wouldn't, myself.'

'Thank you.'

'Look in on your way back — for a cup of tea?'

'Thank you, that's kind.'

Teddy crossed the field, and came out into what was evidently the lane, though it was scarcely more than a footpath bordered by untidy thorn hedges. The gate was a few paces to the right, and Teddy scrutinised it closely, not entirely free from the suspicion that Hamish had met his death elsewhere. The gate was in fact chained and the chain fastened with no less than three old, heavy padlocks. All three padlocks were heavily rusted and showed no signs of ever having been unlocked since the day they were affixed. If someone had let a bull or something into this field, then they had gone to great pain to conceal the fact.

Teddy shinned over the gate, and stood in the snow-covered field in which his friend had been found dead. It was small, half an acre at most; not much bigger than the vicarage garden. High thorn hedges surrounded it and would make the place very gloomy, even in summer, although just at the moment the snow reflected the grey light, so it seemed a bit brighter. There was nothing to see, though, except for a few low banks or mounds here and there which could have been snowdrifts. Certainly there was no way by which anyone — or anything

— could get into or out of the field without using the gate Teddy had just vaulted. He stood shivering, but only the cold was to blame for his discomfort. Teddy felt no kind of spiritual unease apart from the disturbing knowledge that this was, presumably, where his friend had died so mysteriously. He stood there for perhaps three or four minutes, no more — what was the point? There was nothing to be seen, nothing to be done. He climbed the gate again and went back to the farm.

The farmyard was deserted so Teddy made his way to the farmhouse door, which stood slightly ajar, despite the cold weather. He knocked hesitantly, and the door was opened at once by a pleasant looking woman, who bade him enter.

'Mr Lawrence, is it? Come in, do, and sit down.'

Teddy removed his overcoat and accepted a large cup of very strong tea before taking a chair by the roaring fire. Mr Burton, seated at the old oak table, nodded a greeting and Mrs Burton introduced another man, who was very old and sat eating quietly, as 'Jim'. Teddy wasn't clear as to whether Jim was a member of the Burton family, or a farm labourer who qualified for special treatment. Regardless, he ate in a stolid silence.

After a few moments Mr Burton enquired, 'Find it, did you?'

'Yes, thank you.' Teddy hesitated, wondering if it was bad form to talk about such things at the table.

'Gentleman's been to see the field,' said Mr Burton to Jim, who nodded sagely, as if he understood the vague description perfectly.

'Superstitious nonsense!' said Mrs Burton, storming out the kitchen.

Mr Burton raised an eyebrow in Teddy's direction. 'Won't hear of it, the wife,' he said.

'Some won't,' said Jim, much to Teddy's surprise. 'Seen it myself more than once, though,' he added, struggling manfully with what appeared to be a piece of fatty meat.

'Have you now?' asked Teddy.

Jim nodded. 'Cows, sheep. Never a

man, not until now.' He glanced round the kitchen — again, thought Teddy — and lowered his voice, 'My old dad, though, he had a tale, a young lass gone just in that same way. Same way as vicar, I mean.'

'What, in the same field?' asked Teddy, feeling that he might at last be getting somewhere.

Jim shook his head. 'No, over to Docken village. 'Tisn't the field, master, it's them as was in it.' Then he nodded once more, and bent his attention to the plate in front of him.

'Pay no heed, sir,' said Mr Burton — a touch too hastily in Teddy's opinion. 'They're old tales, them. Say anything, Docken folk will!'

'All the same, Farmer Burton,' said Jim, 'you won't go into Docken if it looks like thunder.'

Mr Burton flushed at this, but said nothing.

'You do lose stock in odd ways, don't you?' asked Teddy.

Mr Burton seemed positively relieved at a question he could answer without dissimulation. 'Always losing beasts, sir. Any farmer will tell you that. And the old vet, he can't always tell just why . . . ' He launched into a long tale of some sheep that had become lost, which was clearly intended to change the subject.

Teddy listened for as long as was decent, pleaded another engagement, and returned to the vicarage. He spent the time until dinner — which he would, he supposed, now have to call 'tea' — examining Hamish's books. They proved every bit as dull and soporific as he had feared.

★ ★ ★

Sunday morning dawned bright and cold. Teddy had slept badly, but the breakfast provided by Mrs Oldman cheered him quite considerably. He waited until she had gone — which, it being Sunday and therefore not a 'dusting' day, was not long — and sought out a vantage point that overlooked the church, selecting a side window in a spare bedroom. The room had not been used recently, and presumably not since the time of Hamish's predecessor, and was thus chilly and almost damp. Teddy sat on a rather hard chair in overcoat and hat, feeling foolish — not just on account of his costume, but because he was there at all, on the grounds of some half-baked superstition.

And yet.

And yet his friend was dead.

His friend was dead and neither Teddy nor anyone else could say how he had died.

That was all the justification required and Teddy pushed his uneasiness from his mind and settled down to his vigil. He was determined to watch, but not at all sure what he should be watching for. Dr Hastings had told him that there was no clergyman to take any service at Docken. Those who wished to attend church today must therefore travel the twelve miles to Great Snelling, so there would be nothing for Teddy to see. After some twenty minutes, however, he noticed someone approach the lych-gate which held the stone figure.

Someone who looked familiar.

Mrs Oldman.

It was unmistakably Mrs Oldman, although she was wrapped up — either from the cold or in a vain attempt to avoid recognition. She glanced round furtively before bobbing down to go inside the little porch of the lych-gate, and Teddy could have sworn that she laid something down on the ledge inside it.

He sat back in the chair with mixed feelings of relief, amusement, and contempt — the last of which was directed at himself rather than poor Mrs Oldman. What a fool he was. And no wonder Oldman had tried to keep him away from the stone figure. Oldman would very naturally not want it known that his wife was given to some stupid, albeit harmless, superstitious ritual or belief or call it what you would.

Wait a moment . . . If Oldman wished to distract attention from his wife's innocuous eccentricities, why on earth had he told Teddy to keep an eye on the church? Maybe he'd wanted Teddy to know the truth, and thought that Teddy deserved some explanation of the odd behaviour in the village, but was too embarrassed to simply tell him. Yes, that made a sort of sense.

Teddy found his mind considerably lightened by his perfectly logical rationalisations. He started to rise from his chair, remembering that Mrs Oldman had left his 'Sunday dinner', in the shape of a leg of mutton, in the oven, complete with instructions as to the turning, basting, and general 'fettling' of the morsel. Before he could straighten up, however, he saw Mrs Oldman glance hastily down the lane that led from village to church, then turn abruptly and scuttle off. Teddy was surprised to see another figure approach the lych-gate in the same furtive manner. Once again the figure — Teddy could not tell if it was a man or woman — made a little bob of reverence, lingered a few moments, and then departed in haste. The worshipper was immediately replaced by a couple more figures, possibly man and wife.

Teddy sat down and remained in his seat for two, three, four hours. He watched as — one by one, two by two, or in little family groups — the entire village appeared to come to the lych-gate to pay their respects to what Teddy now thought of as the little stone idol. It was understandable that the villagers should come to the church on a Sunday, he supposed, even though there was no clergyman there to minister to their spiritual needs. They might have gone to say a private prayer or two, but very few of them actually entered the churchyard, let alone the church itself. One or two did enter the building, but only after they had bowed down before the idol, walked back down the lane and used the main entrance rather than the lych-gate. Teddy smiled as he considered the idol. He had a sudden vision of Mrs Oldman dancing naked before the thing under the full moon, and laughed out loud.

But not for long.

The whole village, he realised, was involved in this — what could he call it — madness of a crowd, the sometimes violent herd instinct of the mob. Yet there was no crowd here, only individuals and families, acting as if they had been taking their usual Sunday stroll before dinner. It would have been easier to understand had there been an angry throng chanting or shouting. As it was, this was a private, almost guilty veneration — if that was the right word. Whatever it was, this idolatry was more insidious, more sinister than any angry mob could ever be. Worse yet was the sudden and chilling thought that he, Teddy, was the only soul in the place who had not yet seen fit to bow to the idol . . . No, wait, he wasn't. Mr Partridge hadn't been anywhere near the church, nor had Oldman. They could have been disguised, of course, but Teddy was fairly certain that he'd seen neither of the men.

Teddy looked at his watch for the first time since beginning his vigil. It was the middle of the afternoon already and, rather prosaically, Teddy remembered the leg of mutton in the kitchen oven. As he trotted down the stairs, he became painfully aware of the smell of smoke emanating from the kitchen. He threw the mutton, burnt beyond all hope, into the galvanized dustbin outside the kitchen door. At least he didn't feel hungry. That was one good thing — the only good thing.

He remained outside, irresolute . . . Mr Partridge almost certainly hadn't been to the church, therefore he was very probably immune to the popular madness. Oldman too, was probably safe, but then there was his wife. Mr Partridge, too, was a hospitable sort of chap, had indeed offered Teddy pretty much the run of the manor house should he feel the need. Teddy could say that with some honesty that he felt that need now. He realised that he actually was hungry and that there was only bread and cheese in the cupboard. He also realised that Mr Partridge would, any time now, be sitting down to something rather more substantial than bread and cheese. Teddy closed the door behind him and set off down the lane, not even bothering to glance at the lych-gate as he passed. He went through the village and smiled grimly when he found the place deserted: everyone was evidently indoors. Teddy muttered 'Devotions first, then dinner,' to himself as he passed the Oldman's cottage and set off up the lane to Mr Partridge's house.

Mr Partridge was just about to have a glass of sherry before his dinner and urged Teddy to join him for both.

'I will, thanks,' said Teddy, shamefaced. 'The fact is, Mrs Oldman left me a joint of meat in the kitchen stove, but I rather let it spoil.'

'These things will happen,' said Mr Partridge. 'Mrs Oldman would normally have stayed and watched it herself, but it being a Sunday . . . ' he trailed off.

'Yes, I did fancy I'd seen Mrs Oldman at the church,' Teddy said as casually as he could manage. 'Or, at the side gate, I should say. The lych-gate, where the little stone statue is, you know?'

'Ah. Yes, indeed. You noticed that?' He gave an embarrassed laugh. 'Yes, a place like this there are all sorts of superstitions. The poor folk here don't have the advantages — education and the like — that are such a blessing to chaps such as you or I.'

A thought occurred to Teddy. 'Tell me,

sir, did Hamish — poor McLean, that is — did he remark upon these practices at all?'

'Yes, I believe he did — ah — notice it just . . . well, just before his unfortunate death.'

Teddy frowned. 'But he'd been here a few weeks by then, hadn't he? Do the folk not visit the statue every week?'

'I believe they may, but out of deference to Mr McLean I rather think that they tried their best to pay their respects — as one might put it — when he was elsewhere.'

'I see.'

At last, Teddy thought that he really did see. Hamish was, or had been, a good sort, liked his pipe and a glass of whisky, but he had held very firm religious convictions, as befitted his vocation. Teddy could quite well imagine his friend's reaction to this odd little local superstition, could almost hear the fulmination from the pulpit. How would Hamish's sermon against idolatry have gone down with the odd, blank, inbred village folk? Very likely Hamish had threatened to destroy the stone image by taking a hammer to it. But one of the villagers, or perhaps more than one, had decided to take the hammer to Hamish before he could smash their beloved idol to smithereens. With the cunning of idiocy they had used some method which had left no outward sign of violence — no immediate outward sign, at least — and done away with the new vicar.

Teddy's mouth set in a hard grin. He was a broad-minded, tolerant man by nature, but whoever had killed Hamish must be found and brought to justice.

'Are you quite well?'

Gradually, Teddy became aware that Mr Partridge was looking at him anxiously. 'Yes, I beg your pardon, sir, I am. Just a little distressed when I think of Hamish and a touch disquieted when I think of the whole village turning out to venerate that stone figure.'

'Yes, quite understandable, of course. But you know every village has its holy well, or tree, or something or other.'

'Perhaps, but they seem to take it very seriously here.'

Mr Partridge nodded. 'It's true. I'm afraid they do, rather.'

'Hamish mentioned the figure in one of his letters to me.'

'Did he?'

'Yes. He thought he could detect some inscription on it.'

'Ah.' said Mr Partridge again. 'Did he happen to mention what it might be?'

'Yes, he thought he discerned the name 'Haggai', or something similar. An Old Testament prophet, I gather.'

Mr Partridge smiled suddenly, in a manner that reminded Teddy of a naughty schoolboy. 'D'you know, there's a bible somewhere on my shelves. Shall we investigate?' Without waiting for an answer, he stood and walked over to one of the bookshelves which lined three walls of his study. 'Yes, here we are. H'mm, a concise fellow — as those fellows went! Yes, a good deal about building the house of the Lord, but soon said. Ah, here's an interesting and apposite note. Chapter one, verse nine: 'Ye looked for much, and lo, it came to little.' Might serve as a motto for a good many of us, eh?'

Teddy laughed, the first time he had done so — or so it seemed to him — since he had landed in Portsmouth. 'I fear you're right!'

Mr Partridge returned his bible to the shelf. 'Shall we move to the dining room? Dinner should be ready about now. You know,' he said as he waved Teddy to a chair at the dining table, 'it isn't too surprising that these old beliefs — superstitions, if you will — should linger on in these isolated areas. Without contact with the wider world, people come to rely upon their old ways. I think we've talked about this before, I recall. I gave as an instance the case of the motor car, which, if seen by someone with no knowledge of the internal combustion engine, would appear to be drawn by invisible horses. You never told me about your father's machine.'

Teddy, not entirely displeased at the change of subject, described his father's new acquisition. Throughout dinner the conversation drifted over a wide variety of topics and Teddy was surprised — though he tried not to show it — that Mr

Partridge should know so much of what was happening in the outside world. The meal over, Mr Partridge suggested that they return to his study for coffee and brandy.

'I don't normally during the day,' he disclosed, 'but this being a Sunday, I think we might stretch a point, don't you?'

Teddy, thinking that Hamish would not have objected, agreed that they might.

'I have, I'm afraid, a confession to make,' said Mr Partridge as he poured generous measures of an old brandy. 'I let you think that your observation as to the inscription on the stone statue was, as they say, *news* to me. My family being keen amateur historians, I am perfectly familiar with the inscription. I was particularly remiss in allowing you to think that it was 'Haggai' carved on the base when it is in fact 'Shaggai', with an 's'. Perhaps you have heard the name?'

'Never, I'm afraid.'

Mr Partridge handed Teddy one of the glasses of brandy. 'I dare say not a dozen men in the world have. I am in possession of another book, not nearly as widely read as the bible, but much more relevant to our discussion.' He went to his shelves again, but stopped in front of a small, locked cupboard. 'I keep my treasures in here,' he said as he unlocked the door and removed a squat leather-bound volume.

Teddy looked curiously at the book as Mr Partridge sat down and opened it. 'What is its title?' he asked.

'No title — dear me, no!' Mr Partridge held the book up and Teddy saw that there were no markings or label on either of the covers. 'No, this is a manuscript written by an ancestor of mine. My . . . let me see . . . great-great-great grandfather, I think that's correct, although it may be a generation or two more than that. Yes, here it is: 'Shaggai. A demon of the third rank.' My word! It was all *demons* or *ghosts* to these old fellows, but then they didn't have our scientific minds, did they?'

He smiled as he said this and Teddy thought he detected a note of irony.

Mr Partridge continued, 'Yes, 'Shaggai loveth the thunder and lightning and cometh therein. He maketh men mad, but when he departeth again they think not of him, remember him not, and' — my word!' He looked round carefully, before lowering his voice. ' 'He lieth with women and soweth his seed where he listeth.' ' He closed the book and smiled at Teddy. 'Not, I judge, the sort of chap one would invite to the club.'

'I don't know. He sounds just like half the fellows I meet in my club!'

Mr Partridge laughed heartily, and said, 'Then there follows a . . . conjuration . . . to summon him.'

'I'm not sure I'd want to summon him if he intends to make me mad and all the rest. It is a very interesting insight into the primitive convictions of our ancestors, but I can't for the life of me see why a clergyman would allow a representation of something like that anywhere near a church.'

'Ah, yes.' Mr Partridge regarded Teddy over his spectacles. 'Let us suppose — just for a moment — that one did believe in this creature. Might it not make at least a modicum of sense to have the — *thing* — where one could keep an eye on what might be going on?'

'I recall Oldman said much the same thing to me.'

'Did he?'

'Yes, I had a word with him on the topic.' Teddy hesitated, then decided he might as well be hanged for a sheep as a lamb. 'I couldn't help but notice that neither yourself nor Oldman visited the church this morning.'

'We don't all share the popular delusions, you know! Oldman, I imagine, has his own beliefs. He is, as I think you're aware, something of a healer, with knowledge of herbs, rustic potions, and the like. He probably thinks himself above the local superstitions. As for me, I — well, perhaps I half believe. My family has been here for generations and it's difficult not to imbibe at least a few of the local beliefs, especially as a child. And perhaps those beliefs, silly as they may be, remain with one to some extent over the years.'

'But not enough to make you bow before the stone figure?' Teddy ventured.

'Certainly not.'

'Is that your family tomb, or mausoleum, in the churchyard?'

'It is. A couple of centuries old — no more — built in the heyday of such things.'

'Rather badly damaged at one time?' Teddy suggested.

Mr Partridge frowned. 'Indeed. Even a sleepy place like this has not been entirely detached from the stirring events of history. The Civil War, the Reformation, right back to time when one Stone Age tribe fought another for the land.'

'And the witchcraft trials you mentioned the other day?'

'Did I? Well, them too, then. It all seems very silly to us now, but who can say how future generations will regard us?'

'Yes, I suppose so. I expect that your own family — local squires and magistrates — were very much against the witches?'

Mr Partridge smiled. 'Such records as I possess — and they are somewhat exiguous — are pretty ambiguous. It appears that at times we were for persecuting the unfortunate, misguided wretches who claimed to be witches, while at others there seems to have been a certain sneaking sympathy.'

'I see. Well, sir, it has been most interesting talking to you, and it was very kind of you to invite me to dine, but I should not presume too much upon your hospitality.' Teddy rose from his chair.

'Not a bit of it! Look in any time, please.' Mr Partridge waved at his bookshelves. 'It occurs to me that the late Mr Mclean cannot have had much time to accumulate a decent library and that you are perhaps at a loss for entertainment. If you'd care to take a few volumes for evening reading, please do so.'

'Thank you, sir.' Teddy hesitated. 'I wonder . . . might it be possible to borrow the book from which you quoted just now?'

'Dear me!' Mr Partridge looked positively ill at this suggestion. 'The thing is . . . I know that you'd look after it, but you see it isn't merely unique, so much as . . . ah, somewhat private. The old chap was, frankly, a bit of a reprobate in many ways — for which the family makes due allowance. I'm sure you understand?'

Teddy, very embarrassed, mumbled something or other and selected almost without looking a couple of vellum-bound books which later turned out to be even duller than those belonging to Hamish.

'By the way,' said Mr Partridge as he saw Teddy out, 'I don't entirely like the look of this sky. I think it likely there'll be a thunderstorm tomorrow.'

'Really? One of the famous Docken thunderstorms, unseasonable and all that?' Teddy couldn't help himself.

Mr Partridge regarded him severely. 'Young man, I've lived here all my life, you have not. If it should thunder tomorrow I advise you — advise you as strongly as I can — to stay inside, lock your doors, and don't look out of the windows. But I imagine you young fellows won't be told by an old fogey like me.'

Teddy protested that he held no such opinions and would follow Mr Partridge's advice to the letter. Privately, of course, he hoped that although there seemed no sign of it in the sky, it would thunder the next day, so that he might see for himself what all the fuss was about.

★　★　★

Next morning the sky was in fact very ominous. Teddy stood at his bedroom window for a while, wondering just what to make of it. Snow later, perhaps? No, the clouds were too high and too thin, yet they had that menacing yellowish tinge one might expect in July after a few over-hot days. Despite himself, Teddy felt uneasy, as if the air were oppressive instead of bracing to the point of chilly.

The disturbing atmosphere seemed to have communicated itself to Mrs Oldman and the kitchen stove, for Teddy's toast was burnt and the water for his tea not properly boiled. Mrs Oldman not only failed to notice these defects, but kept casting anxious glances at the sky. Finally, she muttered, 'I'll have to be off now. Best you stay inside, sir,' and hastened away without washing Teddy's cup and plate.

Teddy, much intrigued, put on coat

and hat and went outside. The clouds seemed lower now, the air heavy and stifling. As he watched, a single flicker of lightning crackled down, predictably playing around the lych-gate. Teddy almost laughed at the shopworn stereotype. Almost, but not quite. Another bolt of lightning crackled, this time around the spire of the church. Some localised meteorological phenomenon, perhaps? The effect of the surrounding hills, or something like that; or perhaps because the spire was the highest point for miles.

Surely it couldn't be anything else?

In a mysterious way he couldn't define — as opposed to sight or sound — Teddy became aware of a crowd of people streaming up the lane from the village, through the main gate of the churchyard, and into the church.

Now that made no sense at all. If the lightning were, Heaven (or Hell) only knew how, concentrated round the church, who on earth would choose to shelter there? Teddy made his way to the gate, determined to ask what the devil was going on. But the crowd brushed past

116

him, unseeing and oblivious to his stammered questions. Oldman, too, was there, his eyes beginning to cloud over and resemble the blank stares of the rest of the villagers. Teddy addressed him and received an unintelligent mumble in reply. He thought he could detect the name 'Shaggai', although it might have been his own fevered imagination. Even old Mr Partridge stumbled past, apparently unaware of Teddy.

Two minutes ... three. Teddy stood among the heedless crowd that brushed past him into the church. Then he was alone and through the open door he could make out a low, wordless chanting.

Teddy walked briskly over to the lych-gate. The stone figure was there in its place, though a flicker of blue light surrounded it, looking just like the experiments with static electricity he had witnessed as a student. It was an eerie sight, and he could see how the local superstitions could have grown from a phenomenon which no doubt had a rational, scientific explanation — albeit it one currently beyond his grasp. But even as he pondered the mystery, the blue flame died away, and the stone figure became dull again. Dull, lifeless, and harmless.

Without thinking, Teddy swept the thing up.

It was no great weight, merely a couple of pounds. There was only one way to bring their lunacy home to these halfwits. Clasping the stone figure in his arms, Teddy ran into the church. He pushed through the villagers standing inside the doorway, their mouths opening and shutting as they emitted unintelligible sounds. As they caught sight of the stone figure they fell back. Some were silent, others gave vent to a sibilant hissing. Teddy was considerably heartened to see old Mr Partridge standing in the high, old-fashioned pulpit. Oldman stood a step below, like an acolyte, and it appeared that the two men had been attempting to calm the crowd. Teddy couldn't hope to influence these incestuous clods himself, but he could at least lend his assistance to the efforts made by Mr Partridge and Oldman.

'Here!' he cried, holding the idol aloft, 'This is what all this nonsense is about! Look, it's nothing but a badly carved bit of stone!'

The villagers fell silent, and Teddy felt sure that reason would prevail.

Mr Partridge leaned forward and pointed to Teddy. His bony finger was shaking. 'He has brought the unclean Thing into the church!'

Before Teddy could register what he'd heard, he felt hands on his neck and arms as the crowd surged to seize him. He tried to call out, but someone had already thrust a brawny arm around his neck, choking him. They pushed him to the ground and he realised that they really meant to kill him. Teddy looked up at the pulpit, hoping against hope that it might be some hideous nightmare.

A flash of lightning outside the leaded window threw the shadow of Mr Partridge onto the wall opposite. The old man's mouth was agape in a grin that would do credit to any demon. Instead of horns, his head was adorned with what might have been rank locks of hair, only they were thick, and waved about too much.

There were certainly far too many of them to be arms or legs.

The Burrower Beneath

And in thefe latter dayef we are mayhap grown fomething proude and foolifhe; fhould we not learn from the Parable of the Tower of Babel, and feek not to reach the very ftarf? Our anceftorf in the Golden Age, aye, and in the filver, no great time agone, built unto themfelvef hutf of wattle and daube, and betimef buried their dead beneathe the family hearth, whereon were cooked pottage and meatf; while now we build ever and ever higher, in our finful Pride, while our dead lye unmarked and forgotten in the church yarde, that fhould be hallowed grounde, and no man knoweth what lief under hif fhoef af he taketh hif eafe and eateth hif fupper. Forget not, foolifh man! Forget not thif, that fo high af thy dwelling may be, fo much there if unknown beneathe thy feet; for an houfe if like unto a tree, that hath evermuch rootef belowe the grounde af that trunk above which

121

reacheth to the bleffed Heavenf. And
forgette ye not thif, proude man, that
build ye ever fo high, cometh alwayf the
burrower beneathe.

'How much is this one?' asked Howard
Phillips.

The bookseller, who had been moving
towards another customer like a leopard
stalking its lawful prey, turned and
glanced casually at the little volume:
bulky, bound in dirty vellum, the hinges
cracked, abundant evidence of old
worm; the title hand-written in the tiny
and curled late eighteenth century script
characteristic of 'EC', that great
annotator and collector; *Sermons:
Anon, late 16th Cent.* Worth a couple of
dollars, ten at most. The bookseller's
gaze shifted to the pile of morocco-
bound works on the table that Phillips
had just selected and paid for — and
paid well, too. 'Oh, that's yours. My
compliments. Good customer, and all
that.' And off he went to pounce upon
the poor man browsing through
seventeenth century dramatists.

Phillips took his books home, and — as is the way of collectors — dumped them all of a heap on a side table, while he went out again to a meeting with his bankers. Some matter of a company which had defaulted on its payments to him and others, I think, for this was the late 1920s and business failures were by no means rare. After bathing and taking light refreshment on his homecoming, he turned to the books; primarily to a splendid two-volume set, *A Skeptical Answer to the True Discoverie of Witchcraft*, printed in English in Paris, if the colophon were true, though neither date nor publisher were noted. This perusal lasted the rest of the evening, and Phillips had more business to attend to in the next day or so, trying to save the ailing firm, and did not actually pick up the little volume of anonymous sermons again until the following week.

As so often with books — and other things — the anticipation was far superior to the performance. To be sure, the binding was mellow, the font was black-letter, and there were old marginal annotations (unfortunately illegible); but there was no clue as to author, printer, or date, beyond internal evidence. Worst of all, the sermons themselves were of an almost unimaginable dullness and pomposity, enlivened only occasionally by a passing reference to the Scarlet Woman of Babylon — but even here the author seemed embarrassed by his boldness and quickly changed the subject. The one and only passage of any real interest was that quoted above, about the foundations of a house being like the roots of a tree, which had originally caught Phillips' eye when he'd first opened the book in the shop. This was the sole lively paragraph of an inordinately long discourse on the sins of pride and acquisitiveness, but it held his attention for a direct and intimate reason.

Phillips had always been something of a gypsy and the various curious, and indeed disturbing, events of the previous couple of years had meant that he was — yet again — in new quarters. This time he had settled in rooms in one of the oldest skyscrapers in one of the oldest and largest cities on the East Coast. It was not among the highest, not when Phillips moved in; indeed, at a mere twelve stories (and it really was twelve, there is no missing thirteenth floor in this tale) it was dwarfed by its neighbours. But it was old and prestigious. More to the immediate point, its architect had — perhaps from caprice, or perhaps for reasons of stability — created twin towers, the North and South, linked by a narrow structure which held elevators, ducts, electric cables, and other necessities. From the shape of the building the locals had derived its name: officially 128 West Third Street, it was universally known as the Barbell Building, and sometimes Barbell Tower.

Now the similarity of the nickname to 'Babel' would have done nothing more than amuse Phillips, were it not for another singular circumstance in his new abode. I have said that there were twelve stories, but the first five of these were in fact devoted to offices. Not, *bien entendu*, dubious private investigators or professional correspondents, nor yet surgeons with diplomas from unheard-of colleges who would oblige ladies in their hour of need; but lawyers and doctors of the highest class — discreet, grey-haired men with suits tailored in Boston or London — who would listen sympathetically, promise immediate help, and then as like instruct 'my little man', who would deal with the aforementioned dubious characters. Although the clientele of these men was the very best, still there was a constant stream of visitors to the lower floors. In order that the residents should not be troubled, then, the elevators ran — so far as casual visitors were concerned — only to the fifth floor; the buttons to the higher floors being locked out unless one possessed a certain key. The elevator captains (there were ten or a dozen of them who worked shifts), men every bit as discreet as the doctors and lawyers in the lower depths — and far more understanding — kept one of these keys, transferred at each change of shift. This was solely for the assistance of such residents as had been forgetful, or who were temporarily incapable of using their own key, regrettably a not uncommon occurrence.

Thus far, the elevators do not perhaps seem so very different from a few hundred others. What made them slightly strange — and this was something Phillips had already noticed in an incurious sort of way — was that the buttons below ground level were similarly discriminatory. Below '1' was 'G', which he knew stood for 'garage', though he kept no car and had never been down there; then came 'B', presumably 'basement', also *terra incognito* to Phillips; but then came 'B2' and 'B3'. Beside these last two there was another keyhole. One evening after he had looked at the *Sermons*, Phillips chanced to take the elevator at that curious dead hour between business and dinner. He was the only passenger and the captain happened to be a man called Barnes, a particularly obliging individual. Phillips decided to ask about the buttons to the lower depths, especially 'B2' and 'B3'.

'Well, sir, you'll have been down to the garage? Oh, I forgot, you haven't a car. And of course you don't do your own laundry, so you won't have visited the basement, will you?'

'Is there a laundry there, then?'

Barnes permitted himself a discreet smile. 'The most up-to-date machines, sir. The maids launder the sheets and the rest down there when the tenants don't send them out. And there's storage space too — why, have you not seen your own space, sir?'

'My own space?'

'Are you in a hurry, sir?'

Phillips frowned. 'Not especially. I have no dinner appointment, or anything. Why?'

By way of answer, Barnes pressed 'B' and the elevator slowed in a dignified manner, turned round — so to speak — and glided gently down until the light at 'B' glowed red. Barnes opened the door and stood aside to let Phillips out. 'I'll show you, sir.' He fiddled with the elevator controls to prevent it being summoned without him, and led the way past gleaming washing machines, steel sinks, and cages full of mops and buckets, to a door of steel bars.

'Now, sir,' he said, 'you'll have been given two keys. One is for this door — I have one as well — ' he held it up, 'and one for your own little room.'

'Oh, that's what they're for. I did wonder. I thought they were for the garage, or fuses, or something.' Phillips took out his silver key-ring, found the keys, and unlocked the steel grille. Beyond were a couple of narrow corridors lined with doors, not unlike the conventional image of a gaol.

'You're twelve-oh-three — that right, sir? Over here, and the other key will open it.' Barnes stood by the side of the door marked '1203' while Phillips unlocked it. 'Electric light switch just inside, sir.'

'Ah, yes.' Phillips looked round the little cubby-hole, which was perhaps a trifle dusty, but otherwise empty, and in every way suitable for the storage of such books as might overflow the apartment. 'Capital! I hadn't realised this was here. Thank you, Barnes.'

'Thank *you*, sir,' Barnes pocketed the gratuity and coughed delicately. 'I should be taking the elevator back, sir . . . '

'Lord, yes. Sorry to keep you.'

As they busied themselves locking up and returning to the immobilised elevator, Barnes volunteered, 'Though it isn't my place to say this, sir, you'd be surprised what we've found in these storerooms at times.'

'Oh?'

'When the tenant's died and there's no family, you know, we have to open them up and clear them out.' Barnes lowered his voice. 'I could tell you tales that would make your hair curl, sir! Film stars, big strapping gentlemen that played a hundred love scenes opposite the most beautiful women — but down here, racks of evening dresses! For them — the men. And silk underwear! And pictures, photos . . . shocking, sir, quite shocking.'

Phillips smiled at this revelation, and asked, 'Can anyone come down here? The general public, I mean?'

'Here and the garage floor up above, sir,' Barnes jerked a thumb at the ceiling. 'Lots of clients come in cars, naturally, to see the doctors and lawyers. There's nothing to stop them coming here, but why would they want to, sir?'

'Just a thought,' said Phillips. 'What's down in 'B2' and 'B3', then,' he added.

'Now there you have me, sir. Even my key won't work those buttons, nor yours neither.'

'Oh?'

'I'll show you, if you like.' Barnes inserted his own elevator key, and pressed first 'B2', then 'B3' to no avail.

Phillips tried his, also without result. 'That's odd,' he said.

'It is at that, sir,' Barnes replied equably. 'But then I expect it's pretty dusty, for nobody ever goes down there — or haven't while I've been looking after this elevator, and I've worked here twenty-five years. Not the sort of place you'd want to visit, I guess. Though if you were interested, I expect Mr Aloysius has a key, and would take you.'

'H'mm.' Mr Aloysius was the manager, a peculiar man with very white skin and very black hair, from what Phillips had glimpsed in passing. 'I don't think I'll bother him, thanks.'

At which Barnes caused the elevator to rise to the first floor, where an irate gentleman — who had been detained in traffic — boarded, and implied that Barnes and Phillips were responsible for his late appearance at his wife's side. The gentleman insisted on using his own key and flounced out with a theatrical sigh at the sixth floor, much to the ill-concealed amusement of both the other occupants.

'No tip there, Barnes, nor even a word of thanks! And since it was I who kept you — '

'No need at all, sir. Well, if you insist. Thank you, sir.' Perhaps feeling that this second tranche of largess merited something extra, Barnes volunteered, 'You asked about the lower basements, sir? Well, I couldn't say for sure, but I wondered if the legal gentlemen don't store papers and the like down there. That would explain the precautions.'

'Yes, I suppose it would.'

'Just so long as the medical gentlemen don't store bodies down there, eh, sir?' Barnes laughed heartily at the thought.

'Here we are: twelve. Good night, Mr Phillips.'

Now, as you will have realised, in Howard Phillips the very natural sense of curiosity was developed almost to the point of obsession. After his conversation with Barnes regarding the basements, Phillips began to take particular note of where the elevators were going. Not that he lurked on the landing, but when he happened to be awaiting the arrival of an elevator, he studied the lights as they gleamed bright or grew dull with more than the usual attentiveness, and tried to visualise the occupants of the elevator, their destinations, and their business there.

One evening Phillips had returned late from some modest festivity — a college reunion, I understand — and had a little difficulty with the lock of his door. We are all familiar with this phenomenon and most of us recollect straightening up and staring at the key, as if to reproach it for its stupidity. This Phillips did, and noticed that one of the elevators — not the one in which he had just ridden up — was descending. The light for the garage glowed, then the basement light, then — to his considerable surprise — the lights for 'B2' and 'B3'. He glanced at his watch. It was indeed quite late, later even than the cosmopolitan, and somewhat raffish, inhabitants of the Barbell Building were wont to return home as a rule.

Phillips, now quite sober, unlocked his door without difficulty and went inside. Before closing it, he looked again at the elevator, which still showed 'B3'; the others all showed '1'. Phillips had intended to sleep late anyway, after his celebrations, so he determined to place a chair by his door — which he left slightly ajar — and see just when the elevator shifted from the mysterious 'sub-basement', as he had mentally tagged it. One hour he waited. Two, three, four. His eyelids were growing heavy, and he had all but decided to give up his vigil, when — of a sudden — the light blinked and went out.

Phillips sat up, alert. 'B2', then 'B', 'G', '1', '2', '3' . . . Phillips realised almost too late that it was heading for '12' — his own floor. Hastily he closed his door until there remained but a scant quarter-inch gap, and to this he applied an eye that was somewhat bleary with wakefulness, but otherwise as keen as that of any Pinkerton man hot upon the trail.

Phillips saw the elevator indicator arrive at '12', the doors open, and three men emerge. One was Mr Aloysius; the other two were a good deal wrapped up in dark clothing and he couldn't see their faces. They all went across the landing, without haste, and turned an angle of the corridor so that they were out of Phillips' view. And that was all. He waited an hour or so to see if they might return, but they did not, and he sought his bed for what remained of the night. As Phillips undressed, he reflected that it had been somewhat of a frost. But for all the disappointment it was still odd, for if Aloysius and the other two had legitimate business in the lower depths, why should they not conduct it in the light of day, during normal business hours? But then the newspapers were full of the activities of dark-clad, mysterious men.

The thought that there was an illicit still — a speakeasy, perhaps — in the basement, caused him to laugh out loud as he fell asleep.

It did not seem quite so amusing next day. Phillips was no friend of Prohibition, but he was no admirer of organised crime either. The idea that the basement might be the haunt of gangsters was disturbing. Disturbing and yet curiously attractive in a perverse sort of way . . . intriguing. In any event, it was clear that Aloysius was involved, and so Phillips determined to find out what he might about the strange manager.

Phillips himself was a rich man. Despite the financial turbulence then raging, he had followed good advice from his bankers and brokers, and the effects of the crash on his wealth had been minimised. He thus had no need to turn out to earn a crust each day, and could devote his time to such enterprises as he chose. He therefore contrived to hang about on the sixth floor, where Aloysius had his apartments and his office. After an hour or so he spotted the manager scurrying down the corridor, and lost no time in hailing him.

'Hello! None the worse for your late night, I see?'

Aloysius stopped, swallowed as if with difficulty, and stared at him. 'I beg your pardon, Mr . . . Phillips, is it not?'

'Yes. Oh, you'll have to excuse me, I was trying to be funny. Only I had a late night myself, and I happened to catch sight of you and — and your friends, up on twelve.'

Aloysius was so very pale that he could not blanch, but he did recoil, clutching at the wall for support.

'I say, are you quite well?' asked Phillips, who was not a hard-hearted young man.

'Well? Yes, thank you, Mr Phillips. Only — only I have some business to attend to, if you will excuse me.' As he hastened off, Aloysius added, over his shoulder, 'But I think you are mistaken about last night, sir. I was in my room from nine onwards, and never left it until this morning.'

That's a thumping lie, thought Phillips. And the way Aloysius had been affected was significant, if not downright suspicious. Phillips resolved to watch him carefully in future.

It is, of course, perfectly possible for a man who has no other demands upon his time to stay up all night, but it can present certain difficulties. It therefore occurred to Phillips to check his diary to see if last night was a significant date in any way. It was not, but it was a Wednesday and Phillips wondered if 'lodge' was not held each week on that night. So, despite his curiosity, he went to bed at his usual hour for the next six days.

It was with a tingle of anticipation that he set his chair by the door, itself open just a crack, on the eve of the following Wednesday. Naturally, he had accepted that nothing might happen, that perhaps last week had been a 'one-off', as it were. In that case he had decided he would give the matter up, and let Aloysius do what he would, with whomsoever he would, whenever he would. However, his vigil was not in vain. At around one in the morning the elevator suddenly whined into motion. Phillips was gratified to see

Aloysius emerge, followed by two ladies — or so Phillips, a gentleman by instinct, called them, though he realised that men of lesser breeding might give them a cruder name. Aloysius wore evening dress, and the ladies fashionable frocks, as if they were bound to or from some night spot. Again, the three disappeared round the same angle of the corridor, and Phillips slumped in disappointment. But then he sat up again at the sound of voices. It was Aloysius and the two ladies, accompanied by another two who looked very similar to those of the previous week, both a good deal muffled up and both walking with a distinctive sliding gait.

As they passed opposite Phillips' door and made to enter the elevator, one of the ladies turned to one of the mysterious figures and made a remark, of which Phillips caught only: 'see your face, honey,' or some such. The man to whom she spoke turned away quickly, and the lady shrugged her bare shoulders and pulled a face. She was pretty, but had a vacant look, probably the result of alcohol or some more powerful narcotic. Then they were all away in the elevator. Phillips noticed with a thrill that it sailed all the way down to 'B3', but he was nonetheless disappointed. It looked as if Aloysius was organising — perhaps even participating in — some regular orgy in the basement, which would account for his not wanting uninvited guests straying down there. It was none of Phillips' business, though he did wonder for just a moment what went on, and what it would be like to be one of the company — but only for a moment. Then he put the matter out of his mind and went to bed.

Phillips now forgot about Aloysius, beyond an occasional smile at the thought of the manager's private habits and tastes. But, unexpectedly, his attention was drawn back to the matter by an article in his daily paper. The writer was fulminating against the crime spree taking place in the city and mentioned various outrages: bootlegging, gangland killings, protection rackets, and gambling. Then, in a paragraph on what he called 'the white slave-trade', the writer mentioned the large number of young women who had vanished in the last year or so. The paper had printed photographs of some of them, with the plea that anyone who knew their whereabouts should contact either the editor or the police. One of the photographs was of a young woman very similar to the one whom Phillips had noticed a couple of months before. Remarkably similar, although he couldn't be absolutely sure they were one and the same. He had, you remember, been looking through a slit at the side of the door; it had been rather early in the morning and the lights in the corridor were thus dim; and the newspaper picture was rather fuzzy. Yet Phillips was concerned, and he decided to act.

He had some slight acquaintance with a young man, an Assistant District Attorney, and sought him out.

'Howard, what a pleasant surprise!'

Phillips was straight to the point: 'I say, Dennis, are you involved with this white-slave business?'

Dennis was not, but he knew who was, and introduced Phillips to Captain

Rainer, who raised an eyebrow at the rather disjointed tale before showing Phillips the original of the picture that had appeared in the paper.

'Mimsie Ashburton. Recognise her? Sorry the photo's not too clear.'

Phillips shook his head. 'It's very like her, but . . . no, I can't swear to it. In fact, I suspect it's nothing like her now that I look closely.'

Rainer laughed. 'Yes, I know what you mean. The fashions, the make-up, they all look much of a muchness.'

'Do you know just when she disappeared, though?'

'I'm afraid not,' said Rainer.

'My apologies for wasting your time, Captain.'

Rainer smiled. 'Not at all, sir. Always worth a look; that's the only way we'll crack this one.'

'Is it very bad?' asked Phillips.

'The papers have only printed the merest outline. The truth is that almost a hundred girls have vanished in the last couple of months. Some are — well! But some are just ordinary kids. They come to the city for fun, for money, for reasons no one will ever know; then — just like that — they're missing.'

'Phew! A hundred? Any ideas, at all?'

'No. They could be anywhere,' said Rainer. 'South America, the Far East, or dead; or back home on the farm, married. That's the devil of it: we never get to know if they're all right, which probably makes it seem worse than it is.' He stood up and held out his hand. 'Thank you for calling in, sir.'

Feeling the biggest fool on earth, Phillips went home.

A week or so after his interview with Captain Rainer, Phillips had occasion to return home later than usual, though by no means as late as he had on the night of his reunion. As he emerged from the elevator he noticed that the light of the apparatus opposite showed 'B3', and this reawakened all his suspicions. He checked his watch, noting the early hour. The light blinked, and moved up to 'G'. After a moment it blinked again, and the elevator started off upwards.

Phillips quickly went inside, all but closing the door. The elevator came right up to the twelfth floor and Aloysius stepped out with a solitary lady. This time it was a genuine 'lady'; more, one whom Phillips recognised at once. He had met her just a couple of days before — though even if he hadn't, he would have known her from the pictures in the society pages — Miss Heloise de Coeur, beautiful, wealthy, and independent. What on earth was she doing with Aloysius? Phillips was aghast. Some lady of the night — that was bad enough. But Heloise de Coeur! Still, it was none of his business. If a society beauty really wanted to associate with gangsters — and many did have such an ambition, if what one read in the papers was true — then it was nothing to do with him. Not, that is, until the next day, when the headlines screamed that Miss de Coeur had vanished — apparently kidnapped — though no ransom had yet been demanded.

Rainer himself went to see Aloysius,

together with a sergeant and a half-dozen harness bulls. It was — Rainer acknowledged later — a mistake to take the latter, for at the sight of the uniforms emerging from the elevator, Aloysius darted into his office and locked the door. They heard a shot as they banged and shouted, and assumed he was resisting arrest. He was not. He was evading it — permanently. They took the keys from his body and opened '1211' to reveal a well-furnished, but otherwise empty apartment. There was a slightly musty smell, and traces of what looked like large snail tracks over some of the floorboards. Then they went to the level marked 'B3'.

Rainer and his men found some of the missing girls there, including Miss de Coeur. She was taken to a private mental home, where she refused to go to sleep, babbled of white slugs and things not of this world, and killed herself a few days later when left unattended for a moment. Of the others, three were alive — just. The sergeant was first into the room where they were being held and he, a good Catholic and a father of four daughters, put a bullet into each of their heads. He told Rainer what he'd done and Rainer, when he saw, told the man there would be no inquiry. The sergeant went home and sat up awake with a loaded pistol outside his daughters' rooms every night for the next week, until his wife managed to reassure him. When he confessed to Father Malloy the priest stopped him after the first couple of sentences, and gave him absolution with no mention of penance.

Rumour is usually worse than fact. It was not so in this case, but the rumours — for the facts were suppressed — caused many tenants to leave the Barbell Building. For a time the place stood, sinking further into disrepair and disrepute, the haunt of evermore unsavoury tenants. Then the company that owned the land decided to knock it down and build a modern replacement.

When the day dawned, the crane with the giant metal ball arrived — explosives could not be used as the place was hemmed in by other buildings. The crane driver swung the wrecking ball, intending for a section of wall to be crushed. There was a sort of dull thud, and then the whole building simply collapsed — all of a heap — and seemed to sink into the ground. Of course, the crane driver received a good deal of ribbing from his fellows: 'didn't know his own strength' and the like. He confided to his superiors — and Phillips, who had come along to see the fall of his erstwhile abode — that, 'It was odd, you know, the old place seemed to just go crash. It was as if it was rotten, or the foundations had been hollowed out, undermined somehow or other.'

The Feaster
from the Stars

James Layton was on his way home from work, a stockbrokers on the East Coast, when he paused by the window of a shop. He'd passed by many times before, but the place had changed in the last few days — a not unusual occurrence as retailers felt the bite of the Depression in the winter of 1929. James's eye was caught by the window display, vastly different from the fur coats and expensive shoes he had previously seen behind the glass. Most of what was in there now was, frankly, junk. Old tins and posters from forgotten brands of pipe tobacco, framed prints discoloured with age, and antiquated domestic appliances. James glanced up at the board over the window. The name of the ladies wear shop, '*Maison* Valerie', had been painted out, but not replaced.

He was something of an eclectic collector, and had filled three walls in each of his four rooms with books before he'd married Amy. At least, he *had* been a collector, because Amy didn't much like dust, or the old books which attracted it.

But James didn't collect junk and he had just started to move off when the shop door opened.

A man of about James's own age, mid-twenties, looked out. 'I've lots more inside, you know, if you've five minutes to spare.'

He looked so forlorn that James couldn't help taking pity on him. 'Alright, then,' he said, making a great play of looking at his watch to indicate how valuable his time was. It was a deceptive gesture, for James was only too eager for an excuse to arrive home late, in order to delay the inevitable argument with Amy. It had all been perfect when they'd first met, but now, after only a few weeks of marriage . . . James decided to have a good look around inside.

Sadly, there was little improvement on the tawdry window display. A squat little book with a vellum cover caught his eye, and he picked it up. It was the *Historica Belgica* of Nicholas Burgundus, of which James already had a copy. Still, it might be worth a closer look. No, it wasn't. Not only was the binding loose, but half the pages were missing, there was what booksellers refer to as 'abundant evidence of old worm', and a child had scribbled over the margins with a coloured crayon. James replaced the sad, ruined little book with a sigh. He looked at the proprietor, who gave a sort of half-shrug. James was about to leave, when he saw a curious object on the shelf opposite him.

He lifted the thing down.

It was a wooden carving, almost a cube a foot or so each way, of the sort of gargoyle one saw on the outside of any self-respecting gothic cathedral. Some dark wood, made darker with age; oak, perhaps. It was half-human, a naked male body that reminded him of a wrestler or weightlifter; muscular, solid, squatting on its haunches. The hands and feet weren't human, though, nor was the head. There were claws instead of fingers and toes, and the skull was a cross between a wolf and a lion. The ears were pointed, and the hands — or paws — were held over where the mouth should have been. It looked like something from a medieval woodcut, part wild animal and part wild imagination. Whoever had carved it, however, had been extremely skilful; the muscles almost rippled under the black skin, and the eyes seemed to glow with life.

'How much was this?' James asked casually.

'Oh. Twenty?' James was taken aback, and it must have showed in his face, for the proprietor hastily added: 'Perhaps eighteen?'

'Twelve.'

'I might let it go for fifteen?'

James took out his wallet.

He carried the thing back to his apartment and unlocked his door. From the kitchen he heard Amy bustling about, louder than strictly necessary, and he wondered what the matter was this time.

She emerged from the kitchen and

looked inquisitively at the bag.

'Just an ornament, kind of . . . ' James mumbled.

'More old rubbish?'

'I thought it looked rather nice.'

Amy stiffened as James took the carving from the bag, and then stalked back into the kitchen. 'You know we haven't got the money for such nonsense!'

James hadn't noticed in the perpetual gloom of the shop, but he could now see that the figure wasn't as skilfully carved as he'd first thought. The mouth was completely out of proportion. The carver had attempted to show an upper lip in its proper place, then came the clawed hands covering the mouth, and then — way below the hands — came a row of fangs and a thin lower lip. Had the hands not been in place, the mouth would have gaped open a good six or seven inches. Still, unless one was a student of anatomy, it was good fun. It reminded James vaguely of one of the three wise monkeys, and he wondered if it wasn't perhaps oriental in origin, or even part of a set. He smiled as he placed the figure on a shelf.

James had limited success in trying to placate Amy — so limited that she flounced out the door saying she might not return.

Left alone, he considered his present and future, both of which looked bleak. He loved Amy, and he was sure that she loved him; the real problem was the economic situation. There was nothing he could do but sit it out, and wait until the market picked up. *If* it ever did. James's eye fell upon the carving, sitting on its shelf like a heathen idol. 'Well, old chap,' he mused, 'if you could happen to see your way clear to lifting the stockmarket off the floor, I for one, will be eternally grateful!'

Amy returned shortly. James was delighted to see her and there was a predictable reconciliation, during which James promised that if she still disapproved of the carving in a few days, he would dispose of it.

The following day the market drifted a few points lower.

It was thus without surprise that James

received the news that he was required for a short interview with Mr Vanderboom, the senior partner.

'Ah, James, do sit down.'

'Thank you, sir.'

'Seen the tickertape today? Yes, of course you have.' The older man appeared a touch mortified, but went on. 'You'll be aware, my boy, that most of our rival firms are having to — ah, retrench.'

'Yes, sir.'

'Well, James, we are no exception to the rule.' Mr Vanderboom cleared his throat ostentatiously. 'I'm very sorry to have to say that we are obliged to make some economies in that direction today.'

'Is that so, sir?'

'It is. It is my sad duty to have to tell Messrs Harris and Price that the firm must dispense with their services. I shall be seeing them as soon as our meeting is over.'

'Harris and Price?' James couldn't believe it.

'I fear so.' Mr Vanderboom frowned. 'But it is an ill wind that blows no good.

With Harris and Price gone, you will take over their various accounts — not that they are exactly lucrative at the moment, but never mind. Things will improve soon, I'm sure of it! You'll receive a modest raise — very modest, I'm afraid — and the extra commission.' James was lost for words. 'We'll talk it over at greater length later. Now send in poor old Harris, would you?'

Notwithstanding his heartfelt sympathy for Harris and Price, James was elated at this unexpected turn of events. A modest raise, the prospect of extra commission when the market eventually turned, and — most important of all — the knowledge that his position was safe and his immediate future secure. He stopped at more than one store on his way home that evening, and took wine, flowers, and chocolates back to Amy, who was every bit as thrilled as he was at the news. James didn't forget to thank his carving for its help when she was out the room. He was not by nature superstitious, but he believed the thing as effective a good luck charm as a sprig of white heather or

156

a four-leafed clover.

The next few weeks went well, and financial security seemed to improve relations between husband and wife to the extent James had hoped.

'Remember what you said about that carving?' Amy asked one evening.

'What was that, dear?'

'You said you'd get rid of it if I wanted.'

'Oh, yes. Why do you ask?'

'It really is very ugly — repulsive, even. I've decided I don't like it at all.'

'Oh. I thought you'd grown used to it.'

'No. Now that we have a little more money, I'll go out and buy something more suitable tomorrow. I'll leave it to you to remove it. You did promise me, James.' She smiled seductively as she disappeared into the bedroom.

'Yes, alright.'

James looked up at the ornament. He didn't want to upset Amy, especially after a fortnight of marital bliss, but he was reluctant to part with the object he associated with his recent change of fortune. 'Well, old fellow,' he reflected, 'I don't really want to get rid of you. You helped me out once before, I fancy, care to try again?'

James came home directly the next day, eager to bring Amy news of the first commission from his new accounts. When he arrived the apartment was in darkness, however, and his first thought was that she had gone out. He switched on the electric light and took a fleeting look round. The silence was total, and he wondered where she could have gone. Amy always made sure she was home before him, had even done so before their newfound happiness. James's unease grew to the extent that he did not feel comfortable calling her name. Instead, he shut the door behind him and examined the room more closely.

He noticed the carving was gone from the shelf, and cursed under his breath. Amy must have decided to throw it out herself, although there was nothing in its place, so that too was peculiar.

The bedroom door was ajar.

James pushed it open, switched on the light ... then stopped still, unable to move. The last thing James thought before he fainted was that the carver hadn't made any mistake with the proportions of the face.

His wife was on the bed.

So was the carving.

It's mouth gaped open, cavernous and full.

In The Vale of Pnath

I believe that I have already told you of how young Howard Phillips, after his peculiar experiences in the old church of St Michael and All Angels in the late twenties, moved away from Arkham County, and of how he was subsequently rather disturbed by events in the apartment building in which he chose to live early in the thirties. He moved about for a year or so after the latter, for there was a restlessness deep within him, and at the time of with which we are now concerned he was living in a minor city in a remote state. He was staying at a little private hotel, a situation which was unsatisfactory for a particular reason. Not financial — for he could well afford to buy the place outright had he so desired — but because his books and curios were in storage, apart from one or two choice pieces that he kept with him, and he fretted about them. He fretted for those in store, lest the bookworm should be attracted to the banquet, and he fretted for those in his hotel, lest a discriminating thief, knowing the true value of the mouldy old tomes, should be tempted to ply his trade.

Phillips thus required a bigger place, and for the first time in his relatively short life he thought that a more permanent abode might be a good thing. To this end he left his name with a Mr Dawes, an estate agent. One bright spring morning, Phillips was called to the telephone in the lobby of the hotel, and Mr Dawes — a man of about the same age as Phillips himself — said cheerfully: 'May have just the place for you. Are you free this morning?' In half an hour Phillips was picked up outside the hotel by Mr Dawes, in his car. 'It's an hour's drive,' explained Dawes as Phillips climbed in, 'and the place is pretty remote, so you may want to think about buying a car yourself.'

'Is there a town nearby?'

'Yes, only a mile off, but it's a small place. It has everything you need, of course, and there's a bus station, with regular runs to the city.'

'Then I probably won't bother with a car,' said Phillips, 'though I do like the look of the new Fords.' And since Dawes's own car was last year's model, and they were both young men, there ensued a lengthy discussion of matters automotive, which need not concern us.

What does concern us is Phillips's reaction as they climbed a low hill, traversed a brow, turned a corner, and came to a fine vantage point. Dawes stopped the car and waved a hand. 'Well?'

'Marvellous!' Phillips was not exaggerating, for he had seldom seen a better view. Below lay a valley of fine agricultural land, well-tilled, with occasional patches of ancient woodland, and a little river which held the promise of trout. Low hills surrounded the place on every hand, and a dozen tiny brooks and rivulets babbled down to join the river.

'The locals call it the 'Vale of Pennath', which is a touch poetic, I think,' said Dawes.

'*Pnath*?' Phillips frowned, for the name

sounded odd; familiar and yet strange at the same time.

'Pennath. P-E-N-N-A-T-H. The name of the town, you know, just over that way. And the house too, in point of fact. Pennath House.'

'It sounds vaguely familiar. Have I heard the name somewhere?'

Dawes shrugged. 'It always sounds English to me. The Lake District, perhaps, or else Cornwall? The story I heard was that it was a corruption of 'Pennyworth', because some old chap reckoned there wasn't a pennyworth of folk in the place, or not a pennyworth of goods and chattels — the story varies according to who tells it. I don't know how true that derivation is — very likely nonsense — although the place is hardly crowded, even today, as you see.' He pointed to an old house a little way from the town which straggled up one side of a hill. 'That's Pennath House, the old wooden building. That's where we're bound.' He waved in the other direction. 'The town is spread over the hills there, as you see. About ten minutes walk

— fifteen maybe. Did I mention there was a bus service? Quite good, I'm told.'

'It's a bit remote, even so,' said Phillips. 'Presumably there's snow in winter? H'mm, I think I'll need a car after all.'

'Oh?' Dawes regarded him professionally. 'You sound as if you've already made up your mind to take the place!'

'Yes, I am taking the place — unless the drains are bad, or something,' said Phillips. 'I can see from here that it's exactly what I wanted.'

* * *

The drains, and everything else, were fine. In fact the last owner had installed a brand new bathroom and central heating system, almost frighteningly modern and efficient. Phillips signed a cheque, and the other necessary documents to start the process of buying, there and then. Moving in took him only a short while, and he quickly made the acquaintance of his near neighbours.

Mr and Mrs Graham Harte were a happily married couple in their fifties, lived at no great distance from Phillips, and invited him round to tea on the day of his arrival. The Hartes had two children. Bernard was twenty years old, and at college, though temporarily home on a mid-term vacation. Mildred, more popularly 'Millie', was twenty-two, and lived with her parents. Mr and Mrs Harte took to Phillips at once, he being a polite, good-looking, and well-educated young man, and the junior Hartes were not unimpressed either. Bernard was at that age when a man is inclined to hero-worship. He admired Phillips's car (newly purchased), his moustache, and his pipes. He resolved at once to acquire the first (his father's funds permitting), encourage the second (a hopeless effort), and persist with the third (after several unsuccessful trials). As for Millie — Millie just admired Phillips.

Completely unconscious of the admiration he had engendered in the younger Hartes, Phillips in his turn admired Mr Sorenson. It was while Phillips was sharing a drink with Mr Harte, that the latter informed him of Mr Sorenson's huge collection of old books, manuscripts, and artefacts of a curious nature. Mr Octavius Sorenson was a bachelor of some sixty years of age, who lived on the outskirts of town, no great distance from Phillips and the Hartes. It is perhaps unnecessary to add that Mr Harte himself was a somewhat conventional man, a pillar of the local church, and preferred the ordinary to the outré. Phillips was determined to make the acquaintance of Mr Sorenson as soon as possible and began contriving schemes whereby he could arrange an introduction.

No elaborate scheme was called for, however, for the two men were destined to meet quite literally by accident only a day after Phillips's conversation with Mr Harte. Phillips took a drive out towards the town — perhaps to take the air, or perhaps to buy a bottle of whisky now that the intemperate nonsense of Prohibition had been dispensed with — and the road led past Mr Sorenson's property. Phillips was not yet fully *au fait* with the mechanism of his new car, or so it seemed, for he took a bend in the narrow, winding road a touch too fast, and ended up putting his car in a ditch. Phillips swore loudly as he climbed from the vehicle. He removed his jacket, rolled up his shirtsleeves, and prepared to push.

As he leaned over the hood, another car drove up the road in a stately fashion and came to a halt. The passenger asked Phillips if he needed a hand and when he answered in the affirmative, directed the chauffeur to do the necessary. Thanks and a discussion of the road and the weather followed, and it emerged that the passenger was none other than Mr Sorenson himself. It appeared that he had also heard of Phillips through Mr Harte, and informal introductions led to an equally informal invitation to Sorenson's house the following day. Phillips accepted with alacrity and appeared promptly at the appointed time.

He found Mr Sorenson to be both knowledgeable and hospitable, and positively eager to allow Phillips to see his vast accumulation of books and the like. Phillips found that rather than exaggerating, Mr Harte had considerably understated the collection. You might have thought from his — Christian, shall we say — name that Mr Sorenson came from a large family, but he was actually an only child, his name the result of his father's taste for the classical. The elder Sorenson had also had a large fortune, which his son had inherited and greatly augmented, to the extent that he was in the enviable position of being able to do pretty much whatever he pleased without troubling about sordid practicalities like the state of his bank balance. His own tastes inclined, like those of Phillips, to what we might call the macabre. Mr Sorenson had a purpose-built library the equal of many a small university or college, and had besides a good many rooms in the house furnished almost exclusively with bookshelves to accommodate the overflow from the main collection.

'Books,' Mr Sorenson said, 'are tools; there to be used.' He poured Phillips a generous drink, laughed, and added, 'Proper books, I mean, not fictional trash!'

Phillips happened at that moment to be looking at a row of books devoted to magic. He waved a hand and asked, 'These, too?'

Mr Sorenson laughed again. 'Why not? Oh, not the spells and what you, no. I can't imagine that swallowing a live toad would bring you the woman of your dreams — more likely to put her off, I should think. No, what interests me is this: why should anyone think, believe, that it would work? That's the attraction of these things for me. Trying to work out why people came up with them in the first place, why they believed — still believe, in many cases — what, on the face of it, is complete nonsense.'

'H'mm. I know what I meant to ask you . . . the name 'Pennath', where does it come from? I can't help thinking that I've heard it, or something very much like it, somewhere, and can't for the life of me remember where it was.'

'You probably know that the usual tale is that the discoverer of the place thought there wasn't a *pennyworth* of people here when he saw it. Or that some disgruntled settler's wife — I mean some settler's disgruntled wife — thought there wasn't a pennyworth of use in trying to make a living here. Something of that sort,' said Mr Sorenson.

But something in his tone made Phillips ask: 'And you accept that explanation?'

Sorenson lowered his voice, though the two of them were quite alone in the library. 'Tell me, have you heard of Ptolemy's *Almagest*?'

Phillips frowned. 'Of course.'

'Of course, but have you heard of the *Almagest* of Johannes von Fürst?'

Phillips wracked his brains. 'The Hebrew scholar?'

Mr Sorenson nodded approvingly. 'No, you are thinking of Julius Fürst, but even so, I doubt if one in a thousand men your age would know the name. No, Johannes von Fürst preceded his illustrious namesake by a few centuries, and his *Almagest* is a trifle more uncommon than that of Ptolemy. It was burned by the public executioner of Heidelberg in 1463 and remarkably few copies survive.'

'And von Fürst?'

Sorenson laughed. 'I have no doubt

that he would have joined his magnum opus in the flames, had they caught him. He was pretty much of a pagan and advocated a very unconventional way of life. No, he disappeared under what one must call very mysterious circumstances. Of his great work, only five copies are known to survive.' He paused, then added in the casual manner assumed by the true collector, 'I have one here, as a matter of fact.'

Have you, by Jove? thought Phillips, although he had no time to say it for Sorenson continued immediately.

'I imagine you are similarly unaware of the curious *Chronica* of Baldwin, the renegade monk who was walled up in his cell in Aberdeen on the personal instructions of Innocent VIII — himself a man of the foulest reputation?'

'I fear so.'

'Von Fürst contains only a passing mention, of course,' said Sorenson, half to himself. He stood up. 'I have only a translation of the *Chronica*, by John Maudsley, the English antiquarian, in the 1780s.' He led the way out of the room.

Phillips followed his host down a corridor, up a flight of stairs, and across a landing. They halted before a closed door and Sorenson produced a key. 'My private study. I keep it locked; a bit of dust is a small price to pay for knowing that my real treasures are undisturbed.' He unlocked the door and stood aside for Phillips to enter first. The room was furnished in the style of an ordinary businessman's office, except that against one wall stood a pair of metal cabinets, looking like a pair of gun-safes. And indeed Sorenson said, 'I keep my rifle and shotguns in there,' gesturing to one of the cabinets, 'but in this one . . . ' He produced another key, unlocked the other cabinet, and opened the door to display a half dozen shelves, each laden with ancient tomes. Sorenson selected a particular volume without hesitation, removed it carefully from its place, and set it down on the desk top. He flipped open the cover to show what Phillips assumed would be the title page.

Phillips was astounded to see that the book was handwritten. 'This can't be the original manuscript!'

'Oh, yes. There was a small-scale printing by Jacob Tonson, but the Victorians treated poor Maudsley worse than Oscar Wilde! The Reverend Doctor Jenks, a half-mad clergyman, took it upon himself to track down all the copies he could find and destroy them. He said he'd been personally instructed by the Almighty in order to prevent another Sodom and Gomorrah. A few more of that edition survive than of the *Almagest*, but not many. I don't possess a copy myself, though I've chased one or two false leads over the years, but the original manuscript is some small compensation.' He turned the pages as he spoke, evidently looking for a particular passage. 'Ah, yes, here we are.' He looked at Phillips over the spectacles he had put on. 'I may say that the original *Chronica* was written in a code of Baldwin's own devising, and is pretty dense in places, in consequence of which I differ from Maudsley in my interpretation of one or two cruces. However, the distinction is not usually significant.'

'Please go on, I'm most interested to know what it says.'

'Here is the relevant passage. Maudsley quotes Baldwin as saying, 'And the *deuterotheoi*' — Baldwin's word, which Maudsley interprets as meaning 'the Second Order of Gods', or perhaps 'demons', to which view I am inclined — 'shall come amongst men in the Vale of Pnath, and shall wreak havoc among those who deny them, and shall consume their own with fire, taking them back whence they came.' What do you think of that?'

'Sounds pretty comprehensive, doesn't it? One can imagine wreaking havoc amongst one's enemies, but why consume one's friends with fire?'

Mr Sorenson laughed again. 'I told you it was matter of interpretation. It may be that neither Maudsley nor I have properly cracked Baldwin's code, however, one thing that seems clear is the mention of the 'Vale of Pnath', wherever that may be located.'

'And no clue is given?' asked Phillips.

Mr Sorenson shook his head. 'It may

be merely a coincidence, of course, a similar sounding name.'

'I sincerely trust that's the case!'

Mr Sorenson appeared grave as he closed the book and returned it to the cabinet, which he then carefully locked. 'We'll be more comfortable in the library, don't you think?'

Phillips would gladly have traded a lifetime of comfort for half an hour amongst the books he had glimpsed, but he could hardly admit as much. Instead, he followed his host back down the stairs and into the library, where Mr Sorenson poured generous measures of whisky with a shaky hand.

Phillips had had enough whisky to make him bold enough to say: 'You seem rather disturbed by something, sir. I trust my naïve query hasn't caused you any distress?'

Mr Sorenson managed an unconvincing laugh. 'No! No, not really. It's just that . . . ' He took a prodigious swallow of his drink.

Phillips said nothing in response, merely raising an eyebrow.

Mr Sorenson took another, more restrained, drink and continued. 'There is a strange parenthesis to all this. You see, some thirty years ago — when I was about your age, actually — a curious sort of hobo drifted into the valley here. He claimed that he'd been 'drawn' here, almost as if he were returning to the place of his birth. An odd fellow, too. I couldn't tell his age — you know how it is with these vagabonds, outside in all weathers, no decent meals. He was probably no more than forty or fifty, but he looked older, much older. We're a pretty tolerant bunch of people here, or at least I like to think so, and nobody bothered much about the old chap. Quite the contrary, in fact, they gave him a few cents and some food, and then he did odd jobs in return for meals or a night's lodging in the barn, that sort of thing . . . ' He took another drink of whisky before he said, 'Then things started to happen.'

'Things?'

'Strange things, unpleasant things. Farm animals attacked and mutilated. Unexplained accidents that should never have happened, and never *had* happened. Soon the rumours started and the fingers began to point to this old tramp. I call him 'old', but as I said, one couldn't really tell. Then came a really bad incident. A man was injured by a tractor that, as he put it, 'had a life of its own' — '

'Oh, really!'

'I know, I know, but in a small place like this folks aren't always the brightest. Anyway, the fellow was taken into custody — you've met Sheriff Weaver? No? A good man; I'll introduce you tomorrow. Weaver locked him up, partly on suspicion of just about anything you could name, and partly for his own protection, because there was talk of tar and feathers, if not downright lynching. It was fortunate that he did because — ' Mr Sorenson's voice quavered and he took another drink. 'Because while the old tramp was safely in the local gaol, a child was abducted, a little girl.'

'Good God!'

'As you say. Ruth Mason, her name was. She vanished, on her way home from school.'

'When you say 'vanished' — '

'Vanished,' Sorenson repeated. 'She was never found. There was no body and no trace of blood, or violence, or anything. It was as if she'd never existed. The hobo couldn't have been involved so he was driven to the county line, given a few dollars, and told to clear off. Even that was a bit harsh, in my view, but I think the fellow knew it was really for his own good.'

'There were no other suspects?'

Mr Sorenson gave a mirthless grin. 'I'll come back to that. You see, I haven't told you the end of it yet. A day or so later, the hobo was found in the next county — or what was left of him. He'd apparently burned to death, quite unrecognisable. He was only identified from the bits and pieces he carried around wrapped in an old blanket, his worldly goods, you might say.'

Phillips shook his head, unable to think of a response.

'As you can imagine, the case was investigated a bit more thoroughly than the death of a homeless, friendless itinerant usually is. Weaver suspected — and I half agreed with him — that it was some local ruffian who wasn't convinced of the chap's innocence, and wanted some private 'justice'. What else could it be, after all? There was a tiny possibility — never entirely ruled out, though I never believed it — that it was nothing more than an accident, one of the many that had occurred recently. An old hobo full of moonshine got too close to the fire on a chilly evening . . . I suppose it's possible that it *was* an accident.'

Phillips was rather embarrassed by all this, but said, 'Yes, I'm sure these unfortunate fellows are more prone to fatal accidents than you or I. It's still a terrible thing to happen, though.'

'Yes, of course.' Mr Sorenson hesitated. 'Only — only — my family have owned this place for, oh, sixty years or more? We haven't always lived here what you'd call 'full-time'. My father's business was in New York, and we had a place in Vermont where we went most weekends, so this was for the summer holidays. When I was about twenty-five or so, my father told me a story about a very similar sequence of events that had happened soon after he and my mother bought this place, five or six years before I was born. The same thing happened, or pretty much, judging by his account: farm animals badly used, unusual accidents, and a disappearance, a young boy on that occasion. Once again there was a scapegoat handy, an old coloured man, not too sound of mind. This was a good few years back and things were a touch rougher then. When the coloured man was found burned to death in a shack, some people made pious noises about the Ku Klux Klan, but nobody made any effort to find out who was responsible.

'You think history is repeating itself?'

Sorenson nodded. 'So it seems. Of course every age has its monsters, its night-walkers, its deviants, but it's always struck me as very strange. The parallels, I mean, they're disturbing.' He gave an exaggerated shudder and deliberately changed the subject.

Looking back on his conversation as he walked home later that day, Phillips thought Mr Sorenson probably had a mild monomania, harmless enough, and nothing to be concerned about. The deaths of the tramp and the retarded coloured man were tragic, but didn't warrant further attention from Phillips. So was the disappearance of two children, but there was nothing necessarily sinister in the circumstances, dreadful though they may be. This was an isolated rural community with streams and rivers about, and presumably caves, wells, potholes, and such, just the sort of places to which children were drawn like iron filings to a magnet. The animal mutilations could either have been drunken hooligans from the city, or bored local youths. The 'Vale of Pnath' was an intriguing phrase and an even more intriguing concept — perhaps worthy of a little research culminating in a paper in *The American Journal of Unexplained Phenomena* — but the ravings of some demented old monk were hardly to be taken seriously. There was no need to seek a more complex explanation where a plain one would suffice. Aside from which the alternative was awkward.

Unthinkable, even.

★　★　★

After the passage of a day or two, Phillips thought no more about the odd incidents Mr Sorenson had described, and set about the serious business of enjoying himself in his new home. To begin with, his possessions had to be brought from the various places they had been stored; and since most of those possessions were books, shelves had to be designed, made, and fitted. When this was completed, Phillips began arranging his books by subject, within subjects alphabetically by author, and where necessary within authors, by height, shortest to tallest. One day, thought Phillips, he must produce a proper catalogue of his collection, but that could wait until he was old and grey, and no longer buying books every week. The process of arranging his library was as lengthy as it was pleasant, for each book he touched seemed to fly open of its own accord and demand that he read at least a few of its pages. All too often those few pages proved so absorbing that he turned to the title-page and started reading the whole volume from the beginning.

As Phillips was new to the area, he also received a good many invitations, especially from those families with unmarried daughters. By the same token, as master of his own house for the first time in his life, he wished to reciprocate this hospitality, and began giving modest parties. Having little or no culinary or organisational skills himself, he sought a recommendation from Mrs Harte for assistance. She pursed her lips at the thought of 'some local woman' having the run of Pennath House and Phillips's collection of books and curios, and the result was that Millie Harte acted as hostess at Phillips's first party.

All in all, life was very pleasant for Phillips, with his books and his neighbours for company. He spent a great deal of time with Mr Sorenson in particular, who had generously given him the run of his library — with the exception of those treasures which were safely locked away. Phillips very naturally dropped some broad hints in this direction, but Mr Sorenson always replied only with a man of the world grin, and obviously had no intention of indulging him. Once or twice, however, he made his own hints to the effect that when he knew Phillips a little better, the young man might not find the locked cabinet entirely out of bounds.

In addition to maintaining her role as Phillips's hostess, Millie took to calling for him each day and insisting that he leave his 'fusty old books' to either go for a walk, or a drive, or play tennis. Phillips was not a reluctant participant in these outdoor activities. While he enjoyed Millie's company, he did not enjoy it quite so much — or in quite the same way — as Millie enjoyed being with him. While Millie had privately decided that 'Millie Phillips' would look very well in the society pages, Phillips looked upon her as a lively and likeable younger sister. This difference of outlook did not bode well, but it was not a disastrous difference for anyone as determined as Millie, who resolved to make

Phillips forget his ideal woman. For Phillips undoubtedly had a hypothetical ideal, and the appearance and disposition of this *femme fatale* was far removed from Millie.

At the end of October, Phillips's perfect match arrived in the Vale of Pennath in the form of Mrs Rosalind Mortimer. Mrs Mortimer had skin of a pallor which set the older ladies muttering darkly of arsenic, belladonna, and not going out much except at night. She had long black hair, complemented by her eyes, their blackness not the dead, cold colour of onyx, but the warm, living darkness of jet. Mrs Mortimer was a year or two younger than Phillips, and thus eminently suitable in every way. Or so he thought.

Phillips met Mrs Mortimer for the first time at the Hartes, where both had been invited for cocktails. Mrs Mortimer said something like, 'How do you do?' and Phillips was completely smitten. Despite his interest in antiquarian books and curious phenomena, Phillips could be an exceptionally practical man when the occasion demanded. The first task was to determine whether there was a Mr

Mortimer in the picture or not. Though this would have made little difference to Phillips's long-term objectives, it would have required an alteration of tactics. But it seemed that there was no Mr Mortimer, although it was undisclosed whether this happy circumstance was the result of either divorce or death. Disregarding these finer details as totally irrelevant to his goals, Phillips merely took pleasure in the knowledge that Mrs Mortimer was alone in the world, and began to seek her company as much as might be considered proper.

He did not at first know that Bernard Harte had been similarly affected, though he soon became apprised of the fact. Bernard was once again under his father's roof, due to some small misunderstanding with the college authorities — the precise nature of which remained vague, but had nothing to do with his moustache or pipe. Mr Harte was considerably miffed by his son's untimely return, and even more displeased when he decided to make a damned fool of himself with a woman ten years his senior. He confided as much to Phillips one afternoon. Phillips could only reply that he sympathised with Mr Harte senior, but could quite understand the position adopted by Mr Harte junior. The elder Mr Harte now found himself in an unenviable position. While he would have been delighted to have Phillips cut Bernard out with Mrs Mortimer, he still entertained hopes that Phillips might take Millie off his hands. The entire situation, in fact, seemed set to degenerate into something like the plot of one of the more sickly types of romantic novel.

It would have been better had it done so.

* * *

A few weeks after Mrs Mortimer had taken up residence down the road from Phillips, he was approached by his housekeeper, Mrs Chaffer. 'Here's a thing, sir!'

'Oh?' Phillips had imbibed a touch too much whisky the previous night and was not at his best.

'Terrible doings over at Mr Townsend's, I hear.'

Townsend was one of the local farmers. 'What sort of terrible doings, Mrs Chaffer?'

'I can scarcely put a name to it, sir. Them poor animals, treated like that.'

'Has someone been interfering with Mr Townsend's livestock, then?'

Mrs Chaffer nodded sagely, but could not elaborate as she knew little more than that a number of Townsend's sheep and cows had come to some harm. Phillips was naturally reminded of his conversation with Mr Sorenson, which had been all but forgotten in the intervening few months. It must, he thought, be a coincidence, but he was not surprised when Mr Sorenson called later that morning.

'Heard about these mutilations at Townsend's?' he asked without preamble.

'Only from Mrs Chaffer, whose reports are not always reliable.'

'It's true enough,' said Mr Sorenson grimly. 'I'm going there to see for myself now. Do you want to come along? My car's outside.'

189

Phillips was feeling a bit brighter after a decent breakfast and three cups of strong coffee, so he accepted Mr Sorenson's offer. Fifteen minutes later, they arrived at the farm, and Phillips met Townsend. The man was a couple of years younger than Phillips, and clearly shaken by the events, as he spoke to Sheriff Weaver. His wife looked thoroughly upset, and remained very much in the background, clutching their only child — a boy of nine or ten — to her.

Phillips had already formed a high opinion of Weaver's abilities, but the sheriff could offer no plausible explanation when he was shown the bodies of the two sheep and cow that had been tortured and killed. 'Surely these creatures must have made a considerable noise, being treated like this. Did you hear anything, sir?' Phillips asked Townsend.

The farmer shook his head. 'Nor did Lettie.'

Weaver promised Townsend was that the matter would receive his earnest attention, but it was all he could do. On the way back to their cars, the sheriff expressed his private opinion that it was 'devil-worshippers' from the city.

'Or just devils,' muttered Mr Sorenson in a voice so low that Phillips only just caught it, and Weaver missed it altogether.

Once they were back in the car, Phillips asked, 'Did you mean that literally? About devils, I mean?'

Mr Sorenson laughed nervously, and tried to make light of it. 'Ridiculous, isn't it? To men like us, modern, rational men. But then Maudsley believed it. Superstitious old simpleton, you'll say, and very likely you're right! I'll tell you one thing, though. Mrs Mortimer had best watch out.'

'Oh?'

Mr Sorenson nodded at his own reflection in the car's mirror. 'Yes. She's a stranger, you see, and they'll want a scapegoat when history repeats itself.'

'I can't see that happening,' said Phillips, with a laugh that was not entirely convincing. 'I'm a stranger here myself, come to think of it!'

'Yes, but you're known to be a friend of mine, and of the Hartes.' He didn't say this with arrogance, but with the assurance of someone who has lived in the same place long enough to be certain that anyone for whom he vouches will be accepted by the local families. After a pause, he continued. 'And there's also the initials.'

'I'm sorry, I don't quite follow you.'

'The initials. R-M for 'Rosalind Mortimer', but it could equally stand for 'Ruth Mason'.'

'The little girl who disappeared thirty years ago? Does Mrs Mortimer look anything like that girl?' asked Phillips.

'No, she doesn't. For one thing Ruth was very fair, and Mrs Mortimer is very dark.'

'I suppose there is such a thing as hair colouring,' said Phillips, not troubling to hide his scepticism.

'Now you're making fun of me! Still, it makes me think, even if it doesn't do the same for you.'

'So what do you think? That these children disappear and come back years later, at which point the whole cycle of violence and horror starts up again?'

'I don't know what I think, but I know this isn't the end of it, not by a long chalk. You remember the old manuscript, the translation of Baldwin's *Chronica*?'

'What of it?'

'There's another passage in there, one I didn't quote to you. It goes: 'Except They be summoned, They cannot appear'. He doesn't say who 'They' might be, but one could hazard a guess. I, myself, am firmly convinced that some people are a focus of evil, just as saints are a focus of good.'

Phillips was not to be won over. 'I don't think Mrs Mortimer has anything to worry about.'

★　★　★

A week after the disturbing events at the Townsend place, Bernard Harte burst into his parents' house, announced that he intended to blow his brains out, locked himself in his room, and carried out his resolution using the 12-gauge shotgun Mr Harte had bought him last Christmas. The resultant turmoil may well be imagined, as well as the bitter feelings that arose when it was realised that Bernard had rushed home directly from Mrs Mortimer's house.

Phillips visited Mr Sorenson after he heard the news.

'History repeating itself; I knew there'd be more! And do you see how even the Hartes — intelligent, educated, city folk — are blaming Mrs Mortimer. I told you she had best watch out.'

Phillips could no longer dismiss Mr Sorenson's fears for Mrs Mortimer's safety, and called upon her at once. He found her distraught.

'I cannot understand it,' she kept telling him. 'I'm sure I never gave him to think — I'm sure I never led him on, or anything like that!'

After reassuring her as best as he could, he said, 'I know it smacks of running away, but I think you might be better off moving out of this place until it all blows over.'

'Will it blow over?'

'It must. After the inquest — '

'Will I be required to give evidence?'

'Possibly. But you could let me know

your address, and I could contact you if required. How's that?'

After some persuasion, Mrs Mortimer agreed to spend a few months with her sister in Vermont, and gave Phillips the address then and there. He helped her pack and she left the next morning.

★   ★   ★

A week after Bernard's funeral, and a couple of weeks after Mrs Mortimer's departure, Mr Harte returned early from his morning walk, a little out of breath. Mrs Harte instinctively knew something was wrong, and so it proved.

'Little Billy Townsend!' gasped Mr Harte. 'He's vanished!'

'My Lord!'

Mr Harte paused to recover himself. 'I've just talked to Weaver. He's rounding up a search party. Somehow, I don't think it will be any good.'

'Poor Mrs Townsend!' said Mrs Harte.

'I'll go and tell Howard — Mr Phillips — he'll want to help, I know,' said Millie. Without awaiting an answer she left the house and set off at a run.

Millie turned the corner and noticed the new engine of the volunteer fire brigade before she saw the smoke and flames that billowed from Pennath House.

Mr Sorenson was not surprised when he heard the news. He knew that Phillips had experienced more than one strange occurrence in his young life. He was not surprised at all. 'Except They be summoned, They can not appear.'

Millie took a while to recover from the shock, and married a very ordinary, local gentleman thereafter.

Mrs Mortimer tired of Vermont and travelled to Europe. A year later she married an Italian count.

We do hope that you have enjoyed reading this large print book.

Did you know that all of our titles are available for purchase?

We publish a wide range of high quality large print books including:
Romances, Mysteries, Classics
General Fiction
Non Fiction and Westerns

Special interest titles available in large print are:
The Little Oxford Dictionary
Music Book, Song Book
Hymn Book, Service Book

Also available from us courtesy of Oxford University Press:
Young Readers' Dictionary
(large print edition)
Young Readers' Thesaurus
(large print edition)

For further information or a free brochure, please contact us at:
Ulverscroft Large Print Books Ltd.,
The Green, Bradgate Road, Anstey,
Leicester, LE7 7FU, England.
Tel: (00 44) **0116 236 4325**
Fax: (00 44) **0116 234 0205**

JOURNEY INTO TERROR

E. C. Tubb

The first exploratory expedition to Pluto returns with the Captain, Jules Carmodine, alone . . . What happened to the crew remains a mystery as Carmodine is suffering from amnesia, and mentally and physically broken in health. Later, although his health improves, the amnesia remains. Then, when Carmodine is forced to return to Pluto, he faces a journey into terror. He must remember what happened on that first mission — otherwise the second expedition will suffer exactly the same fate as the first . . .